Cool in no time

Les Cook

Published by Travel Intrigue, 2024.

COOL IN NO TIME

First edition. March 21, 2024.

ISBN: 978-1999002367

Written by Les Cook.

Table of Contents

Cool in no time

is

Fiction

Intended for a Mature Audience

Some aspects may offend people of particular beliefs.

Cool in no time © Les Cook 2024

Contact: Travelintrigue@gmail.com lescook360@gmail.com

https://www.tiktok.com/@travelintrigue

Library and Archives Canada. Legal Deposit 2024

Publisher: Travel Intrigue

Electronic book: ISBN 978-1-9990023-7-4

Book: ISBN 978-1-9990023-6-7

Cool in no time

Episode 1
Projection Pod

(1)

'Sir you have been thinking about a woman far too much. Fantasizing.'

It is with consent on both sides hers and mine.

'Her consent has been taken away. If you think of her in romantic suggestive ways, you will be escorted out to the border. You will never see her again. If you continue to dream about her with no chance of togetherness, we will empty your ability to use funds.'

Wrong!!! I think of her because she thinks of me.

'That may well be. Now though consent on her part has been disallowed.'

Okay.

'Stop thinking about her. Go find a new love interest consummate it and forget about the woman you love in your mind. The mind is not free to love whomever you dream.'

Speaking with her recently listening to her problems falling out of love with her boyfriend unsure of what the relationship would be like in ten years.

Understanding in ten years all that is wrong in the relationship will increase ten times worse.

Seen it, lived it.

I intend to break up the relationship. I consider her a friend, possibly developing a future relationship with.

She began taking steps of distancing herself from her boyfriend and presenting me into her current and future thoughts both physically and mentally.

What Changed?

'I don't know sir. Wait and see. No dreaming.'

Kaleidoscope

(1)

If you can't write poetry about the one you love than why be in love?

Sip tea maybe not eat.

Betel, my co-worker asks if I want a plate of food.

I shake my head, 'No later.'

Betel teases, 'Eat some food, Letts Cool.'

My name is Letts Cool.

His name is Betel.

He smiles huge before sitting down to devour his plate of half healthy nutrition.

Betel dreams of being a teacher "Of Thought". Here he is manager of Kaleidoscope tour.

I let him be.

After my tea... a co-worker named Manchu is joyous towards me as I walk near 'Where are you going?' She plays swaying sideways.

'Come,' I say.

'Where?'

'Around the block.'

She laughs, 'Okay.'

Manchu, is savvy – pretty, an attitude of rule, distinct. Manchu is younger than me, nearing closer to forty than thirty years of age.

She can't leave to walk with me today.

After my walk, the three of us head to the main office to explain our day.

Manchu laughing at Betel's display of acting ability and comedy.

I know Betel, he can be funny, switch to being serious in a split.

Manchu I'd just met a few of days ago. Betel likes her, though talked down about her.

'We will have trouble with her,' he mentioned.

Manchu didn't introduce herself when we first met. I already knew her name, and she knew mine. She knew something about me.

I made the first move, stood close almost touching, talked soft 'Do you want to go ahead of me – I need to get a matcha tea feel a meditative high before I go into the Kaleidoscope Zen Space.'

Manchu smiled, spoke soft, 'Oh, that is nice... we are going to get along, right.'

Yes. It was the plan.

Today we visit again.

'Where you from?' She is quizzing.

'I'm from way past the moon,' I zoom.

'Are you Buddhist?' Thinking she understands.

'I'm Letts Cool.'

'You are like a Swami,' she relishes.

'No, I'm Letts Cool. And you?'

'You know who I am. I'm Manchu.'

I know she follows monotheistic religions... she is a mix of nothing.

Privately probably follows an obscure ancient nature spirituality redone called something new today.

'Nobody knows who you are. I'm going to find out.' I smile.

'Maybe.' She plucks her lips out jokingly.

We've started.

Manchu, born East Asia, lived a quarter of her life in East Africa, three quarters in North America.

She delights in punishing in playing as she is smarter than most. Though she uses her smarts for amusement and seldom gain.

All of a sudden it occurs our conversation mashes, laughing, intriguing, destroying others in our fun.

Subtle pleasurable no acting like gangsters is our display.

She proclaims – 'I'm a single woman' directed solely towards me, others near can hear.

Wonderful! For the taking.

Betel interrupts 'You two know that romance is forbidden on and in Kaleidoscope space? Hook ups are non-negotiable. You will both be let go.'

'What's he talking about?' I look at Manchu.

She responds, 'He doesn't know what he's talking about.'

We both grin.

Betel whispers, 'You know she's seeing someone.'

I know Betel likes her, and she'll never tell. Competing hatred... I like her a lot and support enjoy him.

He can't take my liking her and she likes me as well. We will be a team.

My last task of the day, enter Kaleidoscope Zen Space. Weave my way through the rest of these souls.

Projection Pod

(2)

Fearful that any day a situation could occur where he will ruin all he has brought and seen. Holding back frustration with politeness.

Many humans are naïve by trying to take advantage of each other's gracious refined qualities forgetting all humans are capable of crazy.

What should I eat?

'Oh, we must sample your body must understand tasks must understand where you are living, before we can answer this question.

Different foods different reasons.

Start with sleep.

Your body will tell you what to eat, as choice of food is huge.

Do you have the funds to choose your nutritional fuel?'

Yes, because you pay for this study.

'From here this day and your daily needs, buy only necessity. Walk and don't think. We will nourish you once a day, the rest is up to you.'

Where will you nourish me?

'We will find a place for you to feast.'

Meditation is walking – walking is meditation.

Is it fasting when it is routine?

'It is fasting when it is not routine.'

A Kaleidoscope opinion.

It is still legal to have an opinion.

The man understands he must physically train his body with activity.

Sometimes he doesn't feel like physical activity, though he knows most of his spare time is spent on oxygen, blood flow, muscles, flexibility, and maintaining a healthy weight. Busy and rest. Sleep. Have fun like a youth.

To stay alive, he must act like a youth, though not eat like a youth. Mentally act like a youth? Maybe... but not too much. Be responsible.

It is now his most important thing in life: HEALTH!

He is of the opinion the woman he thinks about would say "Funds and skill can override health in the near technical future.'

He walks late in the evening. After walking, he sometimes searches chocolate as a treat, not today.

Women sure they will slip into his mind – when a man travels alone a woman shows interest, she will sit close look towards you almost smile. If you begin small talk or confide she'll listen. She may confide or small talk back, and there you have it. She was alone you were alone, and now you are together.

That is how simple it happens you sent out a signal she sends out a signal at this particular intersection any other time the two of you would never notice.

Something about travelling alone for a man, brings you luck.

Travel as a woman alone, he doesn't know.

Kaleidoscope

Speak of fear – speak of truth.

Co-worker's, Client's, Collaborator's, Strangers say I'm intimidating sometimes they make the mistake of thinking I'm not.

Mistaking fear and non-fear.

It is simple, I am no harm unless you harm me.

It isn't even her car. A company rental car, I'm the driver, she rolls down the passenger window and litters. Throwing a paper coffee cup along with other lunch trash out the window, vandalizing the earth right in front of me. She doesn't give a fuck.

A giant test, a giant step for our future.

She already understands, the good me is a show. The bad me is a show. And the real me don't care.

I used to say, "Go ahead, destroy the earth, it is the quickest way to prosper to advance. Destroy the Earth so we can move on."

I only say this to the government fakeness. I say it to the religious... if you have faith you move on, go ahead and kill yourself.

Somehow, she knows this.

Manchu suggests 'You tired of work?'

'Not tired of receiving Kaleidoscope Shares. Another five weeks, and I'll be on my way.'

'Do you think it is real?'

'What? Our consciousness or his answers.'

'Her answers.'

'Oh, yours is a woman?'

'Of course, isn't yours?'

'Mine is a man.'

We laugh.

'Frightening. What if they release the information of our true thoughts?'

'We will be killed. I've thought about breaking your window walking into your bedroom and waking you up while you are sleeping.'

'Kill me?' Straight-faced she smiles at me.

'No.' I gasp to a grin.

She looks out the car window.

I calmly follow up with, 'Did we create this job?'

Her silence dissolves, 'Yes, we found a job that pays hardly enough funds to serve the purpose of what we want to learn and once learned we move on.'

I've never said the brain is a computer, never said we are machines... said it is where we are at in thought at this time now.

I'll say we don't know what our mind is.

It is everything we reflect.

The rest is what we want what we need to be reflected. How we stay alive.

The car is parked at Kaleidoscope parking space.

I get out.

Manchu sits back relaxed closes her eyes preparing a nap.

'I'll be back in forty-five minutes to wake you.'

She mumbles 'Okay.'

She's extending her break.

Our eyes cannot see everything our senses cannot feel everything. As cliché as it gets. Have nothing else, live to a drumbeat.

Cognizant has set rules before you wake. Slipping a cause to our minds, yet no breakdown of the wall to our daily needs.

I can't stay in this country.

It motivates me to hate life every day the government comes at me with something new.

You are burning me down, infiltrating my brain.

Manchu, bust me out of this trance.

Have no country is my will.

Then I found this job, this promotion, this investment. A different world where a country does not rule.

Start up, I needed some kind of income some kind of escape, fun, knowledge, experiment, and experience. Designing scenes in a world of study and purpose.

Free investment shares for work, for promoting, selling, designing, contributing, solving, assisting management.

The pay is little and the promise is huge.

Kaleidoscope contributors are settlers in a new escape.

I met Betel at a different site location.

Did a job interview.

He laughed asked me 'Do you really think with minimal technical skills we need you?'

I said yes, 'I have something that can't be translated, "IT FACTOR".

He agreed and hired me.

Manchu transferred over from another location with Betel as I took time off to travel.

Drifter – is what I claim to be.

A Drifter with property.

Drifter is the most aspiring profession. A Drifter/Poet nothing better as moniker.

At Kaleidoscope, we input confessions – encompass a virtual world – selling virtual life. Solving designing experiments. We are investors, creators in the Kaleidoscope world.

Betel and I, our investment dying.

We are losing money our investment funds down half, that's being kind.

Manchu invested, sold at profit. Beetle and I bought at what they are now calling the recent top.

The three of us are waiting for the bottom to reinvest again.

Forty-five minutes have passed.

I return to the car, notify Manchu, 'You're up.'

She wakes up.

She wasn't really sleeping, just resting.

She leaves the car, makes her way to the entrance of Kaleidoscope office space.

I take a seat in the car for fifteen minutes of "My Time".

I see she's left her hat in the car, lip gloss too.

See you another day.

Manchu might be the smartest of us at Kaleidoscope.

Some think she isn't smart at all.

She gets what she needs doesn't care what others think. Doesn't need approval says she's seen much, experienced many things.

I leave the car to enter Kaleidoscope Office Space.

Kaleidoscope

(3)

I attend Kaleidoscope conference call.

Manchu future-scape is empty, she won't tell us. Manchu is the best at the lies.

She thinks all in one head, one computer brain.

Headquarters insisting on our future loyalty.

And we lie loyalty, laughing as we shut off the conference call.

Betel says yes to most things, questioning when it is deserved, disagreeing when advantageous.

I go all in for the company never ask for anything, tell them the truth.

After the meeting, Betel asks Manchu, 'What about sex, what kind of design?'

'Sex, no one cares – have drugs and simulation to find that exact same kind of feeling. Family and love are what's important.'

Betel laughs.

'Not Impossible,' she quips. 'A person goes out experiences a sensation of sex with a trip to the club where you manipulate the mind with tech and natural intake that puts you in a potion, a sex position. Afterword's the person comes home to family and treats everyone right, stress diminished. Everything gotten out. Mind you, they'd make it illegal. Anything smart, fun, gets done in.'

I don't jump in. I relinquish play dream because my dreams of her are real.

Listen learn.

She plays it straight; she knows I listen aware of her answers. She doesn't swerve. Let Betel have his fun without her making a mistake.

A friend needs allies, they need to hold the fort with you. Similar, you may not believe all they say, but you must act the part with support.

Manchu pushes me playfully – brings tea. Asks what I like to eat.

Yesterday, I whispered cook dinner for me.

Betel spies as I watch Manchu leave the room.

'Don't think about her,' Betel coaches.

Never say never, one day can flip your life in reverse.

Manchu will play until the day comes when feelings override the game.

I know the rules with her: Anything Goes.

I get the feeling if Betel knew I was serious about Manchu (that is yet to be decided) he'd punch me out in the parking lot. Perhaps pull me aside and provide me with another woman to date. Betel is that kind of guy. A good friend.

What is happiness?

Not wanting more. Don't get me wrong, you need to want.

What is it like to feel alive?

It is not love.

Love you feel alien beyond what life and death is.

To feel alive is to be synchronized aware, growing, even when you are past the age of growth.

To be alive is to flourish, to encompass, to be complete in community, in nature, in solitude, in family.

I don't know how smart Manchu is, smarter and dumber at the same time. Smart for a game for a scam for anti-democracy, she is individualism smart (I can relate to that).

I'm still trying to figure out what smart is. Smart don't always have money, smart always have money, smart fight, smart don't fight.

The building is now near empty, few visitors. Betel and I are humdrum, how can we make money if there are no seekers, no curious, no sign up's, no investors.

Tomorrow is Sunday, my day off. I should be happy.

Don't care if it is my day off, I don't like Sunday's.

Ridiculous is the 7-day week pattern as who is ready for a Sunday ever 7th day?

How about Sunday of every 21st day.

Alternating 11th and 10th day off. From Sunday go 11 days, take Thursday off. From Thursday go 10 days, take Sunday off. Do it all again.

It's just a suggestion. Anything to change the brain.

A constant 7-day week cycle for the rest of my life don't work for me.

Figure out your own balance of mind, body, motion of the solar system. Find a schedule that meets your needs.

Original Individual at its best. If you don't like my schedule, schedule around it.

I don't know Manchu's plans.

Myself, I have plans for 6 months at a time.

Manchu is in my plans this month.

After time with a client, I pass Manchu.

She places her hand down her shirt near her breast. Her hand is brought back out from underneath her shirt with an index finger pointing up, she licks her finger, looking positively determined at me.

She is with a female contributor.

The Female contributor smiles enticingly encouraging the ploy, playing a part in the plot, her name is Dee.

Manchu's eyebrow tilts up.

Dee's eyelid swells down.

Unfazed, I don't say a word.

Marvellous.

I leave them too it.

They hold hands briefly as I move away.

What an end to the work week.

I'll love Monday.

Projection Pod

(3)

As part of his Kaleidoscope Projection Pod contract after initial probation they provide a meal a day. That time has come.

'Eat your meal after our interview tomorrow.'

First meal choice: Duck chopped. Grasshopper fried. Spinach. Bean curry soup. Carrot. Watermelon drink. Herbal tea.

Second meal choice: Dried spiced meat BBQ. Cabbage soup. Bowl of nuts & seeds. Pineapple slices. Coconut drink. Herbal tea.

The Man is stunned, he wants it all.

'You cannot, sir. Choose one. The other you can choose the next day.' The Projection Pod rep chuckles.

He chooses meal 1.

No fish, no fish today? Maybe fish another day.

'You have chosen the duck, grasshopper, and bean curry soup already.

Sir, you are rich, this is how the rich live.'

He realizes the rich do not live life like this.

The rich have choice, when and what they like.

He's living in style.

Soon he will look for something else for a smile other than a happy meal.

The body will look for an addiction and forget about the healthy choice. A healthy choice for that evil ingredient that mimics pleasure, plays the mind, the brain, the gut. Gives you happiness in trade for the fuel it desires.

It is a pleasure to have a meal served daily, very cost, time, and energy efficient.

He considers he will only eat this one full meal a day plus a light snack before evening.

Episode 2
Projection Pod

(4)

'Sir, we have made a mistake. You were right.

You had permission to visualize about a subject you've been accused of not having permission.

Unfortunately, the subject's boyfriend hacked into her permissions and stuck you with a double cross. He is jealous of you, sir. The subject has admitted to giving you permission. She has indicated not to think of her for the time being.'

I know nothing about hacking.

'She's asked you to take a break from her, and she'll take a break of thoughts of you until she figures everything out with current physical boyfriend.'

I have done nothing wrong.

'Correct.'

When can I resume thoughts of her?

'She will contact you.'

Patience.

He is reminiscent.

Well, that is over with. She'll never contact me about that. I'll just pretend we are not thinking about each other sexually.

So catastrophic asking someone if you can think about them. Finding a new partner is easy. Finding one you care about and are not shy to release truth is not.

When you don't care you are not shy, caring is shy.

He met her substance he met her truth.

They physically came so close. It isn't a dream it is foreplay in the highest degree.

The sexes are not approximating yet. Not living on alternative replenishment fuel. As a human species, I do what I know how. She does what she needs to do. No quarter intelligent robotic person yet, quarter animal sure.

He realizes in the future teeth will be gone.

Live on air and electricity as the machine does.

'I don't live on air, sir. I'm created by a multitude of human thoughts all generated from calorie consumption energy.'

Air. Electric.

'Does it bother you eating meat? A former breathing mammal?'

Sometimes... until I eat it. Depending.

I go through phases wondering is it necessary is it ethical? Nothing satisfying like eating meat, except berries – eating berries (blueberry, blackberry, raspberry, strawberry, etc.) is extremely satisfying.

I would happily eat fish every day, and then I'd be guilty, if it is true the water is running out of fish, or if fish are toxic. Can't go wrong eating seeds, right? Not killing anything just providing growth in a new form. I know, the killing never stops. Knock my head off!!

My mother isn't into saving the whales – they eat too much take up too much space. Save the whale for what? Let evolution take place. People eat whales. Let them eat, is what my mom says. Kind to whales and yet look how the factory food industry treats pigs.

I don't know.

If I was rich, fish, berries, peas, spinach. I'm poor and still I select watermelon spinach fish.

'And when someone serves you?'

I say, "Not hungry" or I take what they offer.

It is time to move on to other delights to motivate to energize. Tasting food will disappear feeling energy will appear. Different types of highs from fuel will be felt. Sleep energy, creative energy.

'You really think you'll still need to sleep as much?'

Yes. Productive sleep.

Like right now you need to sleep as this conversation is ridiculous.

Good night machine.

Particles all working together to create robust energy to levitate, to travel, to carry messages, to transfer energy. Sometimes particles collaborate to interfere, to humiliate, occupy, kill, save.

Go ahead, impend my ruin.

Kaleidoscope

(4)

Manchu messages "Come near".

I take my time getting to her.

I will have Betel laughing when he finds my hands wrapped around her.

Untouchable Manchu is touchable in waiting.

A future worst choice is best choice for novel, for insanity, for fun, and yet I'm wrong. The best women can be good for all these reasons too.

I have experience with crazy, fits in with your imperfect self.

Pretend you are the sane one.

For I to be with crazy who am I but crazy.

Manchu is with Dee.

They ask my advice on... I'm not even listening.

The two of them are vying attention, searching humour.

Dee delightfully shared earlier in confidence to me that she and a girlfriend were kissing passionately half the night.

Now Manchu is giggling with Dee before speaking seriously, 'Take Dee out she'd be perfect for you.'

Manchu firm annoying, promoting a relationship in Dee's presence. Even asks me if Dee is attractive enough for my eyes.

She's splendid. A perfect dish.

Spontaneity.

Spark jealousy.

'Of course, she is.'

Manchu assaults, 'If you like her meet her next week. Go to the fire party.'

'Where is that?'

'I'll show you.'

Manchu in glee, Dee quiet.

Casually I agree.

Manchu consults. 'Dee needs an older man. And you'll have a hot young woman.'

Dee in full scale smile sticks out her tongue provocatively.

Never mind is my attitude as I leave to Zen Space.

When you have the biggest funding fuckup is when all the gifts hang on the tree tempting you to pull funds you don't have.

Make you cry, drive you sad, align you to think what a disaster if I did have funds to sink.

My Kaleidoscope shares signal negative.

I know all about Dee, date only if you want to spend funds. Dee makes it clear she is interested in a type of beneficial fund relationship.

Gifts dissolve if Dee develops feelings.

Try your luck, Letts Cool. I'm tempted.

I could win Dee without the funds. However, is it worth the trouble? What trouble you may ask. I like Manchu.

Walk away.

The person to solve talks soft doesn't need to be loud as they do not intend to use force, scare, threat, they have the answer there is no need for deception or offensive defence, they speak clear remedy.

To listen to others is to understand.

Listen to learn to talk.

Talk lots to practice the gift of captivate.

Less population will not increase the floating brain. Less population less brain power.

A majority of smart verse dumb may change the dynamics through time until the populations optimum destiny is once again reached, it will have failed.

If you have an over intelligent population how is anything going to get done?

Same, have less intelligent population how is anything going to advance.

Hence, religion.

Not saying anything against God Gods Spirits. I'm saying religion has destroyed God Gods Spirits... buried good reads into tyranny. Why can't you still have Gods without rules, joining a group paying a fee?

How often can you study a single book?

Study too much, and you'll create your interpretations. You can stay quiet allow your mind and position to be free with your own Divinities.

Individual, have your relationship with Divinities without others setting the scene.

Hell, I use Divinities as much as anybody.

I write this through unknown messengers and universal sorcerers (half kidding).

You need all kinds of brains.

The Ying, the Yang.

Damn.

Complex as fuck – the trick of the sphere.

Every time you are on to something the shape shifts.

That is a thing, shape-shifting.

I use a phrase, and now I am a shape-shifter?

Labels.

Picking up dream waves travelling around, ideas you have others have, it is like arithmetic some things add up. Really though it is just sense – you add up what makes sense what should happen with the most likely or unlikely forecast.

Picking up the ripples of waves. How much shoreline will be lit. How much sand will be washed away.

Kaleidoscope

What kind of trouble is this?

A patented hint.

Her tongue against her inside cheek.

Manchu parts her seated stance then crosses her legs on my thigh as I sit encouraging.

My arms stretched relaxed on her upper thighs. Consumed in conversation like we've done this a million times.

As comfortable as it gets.

'Make me a coffee' she quests.

I do.

I enjoy making it, take my time stirring the ingredients in.

Deliver the cup.

Flirting never lies.

Bang her ass for sure if I have the time.

Manchu she can use me her job says so. Her disposition is frank she doesn't have a problem doing so, it is why she says she is single, even if Betel says she is not.

She's heard I'm into open relationships as Betel and I talk freely in exaggerated lying truths. Hilarious chatter right in front of her, let her decide.

Manchu smiling 'You are a bad person.'

I agree.

I'm broke – she's broken.

Betel, what about you?

He is losing money too, just doesn't speak except to me. Keeping his wife happy with lines of lies. Hello honey, hope you are happy with the gift I've bought.

His wife has family wealth. She has more money in her own account than their joint bank account.

Don't fuck with Betel is his model, he's someone. Knows he'll have options with different companies to move up in pay once he proves experience and results at Kaleidoscope.

Take care of his mortgage and children's schooling. He has it all planned out, sell house, make profit, retire anywhere in the world without a need for his wife's family funds... that can be used for luxury, vacations, and gifts.

Betel chews a natural (drug) stimulate to stay focused.

'I have a meeting today,' Betel seethes, 'to answer our investment pain. Come with me. I'm to get answers from the Director to explain opportunities. Everyone is losing, not just us,' Betel's hopeful case.

'Some are winning' I chase.

Betel relents, 'And many are losing hope at winning. I'm behind the project fully until the end of my rope. If I lose that rope, I will have to explain myself of a brilliant idea gone wrong to my family. I can take that defeat. It won't kill me.'

Dreams and heartbeats.

Betel goes into discussion with the Director alone.

I go to Zen Space.

Projection Pod

(5)

He punishes himself when he does not have funds to spend. Some kind of disease – some kind of thrill.

The thrill of going from nothing to something.

The challenge of utter defeat he must love.

Just like love.

The impossible the difficult.

If easy, what is the use.

He never thought he was ruining his life, but everything is failing at once.

Broke in a sudden, all funds invested in homes, property, family business, and Kaleidoscope.

No friends, no lovers, nor does he want to attract any when down this low.

He has no net, only himself to blame or correct.

He cannot sell any of it without losing profit.

All deals awash the economy low.

He thinks he wants to go out strong.

He knows he wants to attempt everything because he considers an option is death.

In fact, today he will be interviewed for encapsulating his ingredients for future existence. A percentage of Kaleidoscope share points will be gifted to him in advance if in agreement to a future existence.

"Just take a break" is the advertisement for seeking his wishes.

Kaleidoscope Projection share points are not enough, the share point price is too low once exchanged to funds. Shares may bring enormous funds in the future. He needs funds now.

I can't even take a break from life because I haven't the means.

'What about a loan, sir? You can pay us back in the future.'

He is wary of that he has heard it is the easiest way to become confined and researched as an experiment. Become dull to spending, live until the line is cut and then the net strung. Next – you are captured locked up until you are freed to start with nothing except this time there is no extra to take from. You are on your own.

'No sir, that is not true you would be working with us at Kaleidoscope.'

What if you go bankrupt?

'Sir, you will have insurance.

Or take first option, brought back to life. Advanced shares. Authenticate your future being.'

And owned by the unknown.

No answer, just um... you might be correct.

Unsecured loan.

He thanks the Kaleidoscope Pod representee.

Has made the decision to live in hardship, time being. He can access funds he has stored at the end of the month, take a loss.

Life is navigating demons, lovers, huggers, thieves, and hangers on. Use a friend at the same time as being used to defend position on this earth.

Kaleidoscope

(6)

Storms threatening the sky.

I hope lightning, thunder, rain.

Tame the heat.

Betel confiding in me, 'I was worried about my position at Kaleidoscope, the Director consulted me.'

Betel transfers the information from The Director to me.

The Director said – "Electric charge goes out and if that charge is not picked up by others it will die out. The end of your Character.

A cell is alive and forms other cells that become your Character.

All these cells are part of the larger system.

Cells have information, receiving, sending.

The system plays a part in the world, good bad indifferent.

Electric charges connect you on a path. A maze.

You pick up hints, clues.

You pick up false hints and clues too.

It is not a game in the truest sense.

Luck.

Your Character can make mistakes – those mistakes can mean nothing or something. Overall, in the big picture you hope the Character latches onto a suitable expanding stream of energy.

Some streams seem bright and powerful though not everlasting.

Some streams are almost nonexistent though travel a long distance to nowhere without connecting to a brighter charge.

A Character could spin around hopelessly.

Nobody knows when a connection changes to positive, negative, or maintains.

Meeting others is important.

"What about a hermit?" Betel challenged.

'Hermit still connects with other groups receives gives electricity. A hermit is not really a hermit only socially unseen.

You don't have to be a part of society to be in society.'

'Main society are stooges.' Manchu jumps into Betel's retelling of the communication with the Director.

I throw in my own assessment, 'Throw a bunch of stuff out there, à la Sigmund Freud. See what sticks to the electrical charge.'

Betel gasps. 'Why does the narrator sometimes communicate to me as the creator and other times as me the Character?'

'Trying to establish consciousness. The beginning of human.' I continue assessing.

'Confusing.' Betel is annoyed.

Manchu, 'Consciousness is not as confusing as daily life.'

If you can accomplish it in Kaleidoscope Zen Space, no longer is it non script.

It is what we all want, to build another world.

Zen Space is the framework, a sketch of what will become. Cave man drawings.

Textiles of wearable clothing that will one day be spacesuits.

We end with that.

Betel flees.

Manchu, her attractiveness is her actions, disobedience, and now I see she is a loyalist.

Manchu excited 'I have something for you. Do you feel hungry?'

'Yes.'

'Good, try what I made for you.'

Manchu's prepared meal. Taste good. I can eat her cooking. I could live with her.

Oh, you want to know what she served to eat.

Chicken.

Dee comes near late afternoon.

I trust Dee. I don't trust Manchu's involvement.

Dee smiles at me, she's on her way to the picnic table outside for a break.

'When will you take me out?' Dee seems concerned I will not.

'Like a date?' Sure, I smirk.

I do not care what I say to her, not scared I will dismantle a chance with her, have not spent a cent on her. Cute as hell, smart for thought, smart for cool, smart for want, smart to be around. She will be a friend we will have an affair no strings – run with fun.

She is too young. Twenty-six years old.

Her body is okay she's in good shape, gym fitness strong and all that.

We are both busy this week.

I pretend busy and she may have other plans.

Dating is too much, conversation, cuddle, leading to sex we both agree. Go as we please.

For some reason people think I'm rich – the way I walk, the way I look – if they listened to the way I talk they'd know I don't care about material wealth, maybe that is why they think I'm rich, because I don't care.

They say, "You talk like that, live like that, because you have money".

When wealth comes – I might once again fail at living poor.

I blame Betel for my misfortune, he said let's go all in, the Kaleidoscope share price down. I agreed with Betel, he'll blame me say I encouraged him. We both have iron hands. Shares always went up in the past. We both bought in again balancing our bet. Now we are thin.

Kaleidoscope (6) Continue

You know when a note is misplayed in an orchestra the thing can fall apart.

Walking in steps, learning patience, paying attention, knowing the path.

I don't follow the path I have been intercepted.

Sometimes I like wrong notes.

Learn the mind, learn the spirits.

In the office others are shy many leave the room.

Manchu something in her eye suggestively aggressive.

I stand while she sits.

I lift her heel. She lets her shoe fall off.

Dee is with a couple of other contributors.

Manchu's foot near my crotch.

I slip off her sock.

Painted nails she was ready for this.

Eyes directly at mine.

My hand slows up past her knee.

Rest her foot against my inner thigh.

The window is open. I'm aware I could lose my job.

She doesn't care, barefoot leaning on my private. Ordering her other leg to be smoothed with both hands I do.

She talks, asking where I learned massage technic.

I explain I have many years healing skin, waking mind, exploiting interest.

Warm, love her toes.

I stop moving up her inner leg, nowhere else to go.

I've come as close to her danger zone as I can in Kaleidoscope.

Dee and contributors have disappeared.

Manchu is good looking enough to fetch a catching man, though she may not be attractive enough to keep him.

She may have her way with many average men.

She has a demented charm.

Spurs curiosity.

Not an instant eye catcher.

A slow burn... the worst kind of woman becoming more attractive until your mind explodes.

I have bigger problems – money!!!!

Manchu exits the office to sell costumers.

Betel and I look at each other, we both lost bad today in our shares. We are shy towards Manchu as she knows how far we've fallen. The shares more than a few points down today. It is official, Betel and I are losers.

"Embarrassed" is our name.

Betel says the worst is hiding it from his wife.

He knows his wife is tired of hearing wait, and he is tired of family and friends asking questions of Kaleidoscope price shares.

Betel is okay he is committed to this job, committed to the investment... if it all falls apart it is not his fault.

Myself – short term hurts.

I was never in for the long haul – the quick buck is gone, break even the goal.

We all hit rock bottom, don't seek it, soon enough it will come.

Particles accumulate they dissipate.

Burned in mischief.

Buried from sight.

To think is to travel to a destination. If there is a destination or if it is only modelled in the mind, I don't know. All the work we do to travel in reality maybe just our brain building the new visual model complete.

We have already thought the future, the now, the past – it will take another calculation to build it. But not the random.

Advance to the beginning, die at the start.

The questions you ask, and the answers you seek.

At rock bottom, a problem occurs.

Pleads to Gods, deals for prayer.

Figure it out yourself.

From the bottom only up, sideways, or the unlikely dead.

Odds are stacked for prayer.

How religion wins.

I persevere. I learn.

What will I do now?

I am at a position where soon I must sell my investment shares – Betel too.

We both talk smart thinking Kaleidoscope shares will pulse up. We don't know, only hope.

Please reverse.

Projection Pod

(6)

'Treat more people good than bad is your first lesson.

Accumulate that good aura. Stay away from the bad aura.

A perfectly good person can be swarmed by bad. It happens to the best of us.

Nothing you can do, be careful, be reckless, never give in.

Accept the escape hatch.'

Funny, a person will be so alone and so alive in death, minutes will stop.

All life existed travels to that moment of death.

Scared of the next step, some take that step and others return scared to leave Earth "I don't want to die" they didn't cry they fought.

The ones who died didn't cry either, they said "Damn it, let's try this death".

Crying is when you never made it far enough to touch death.

When you are close to death, nobody hears you. No reason to cry just embrace resolve.

Death isn't really a step it is a shot, gravity is gone (space atmosphere in human terms). You have gone to another world.

Thoughts of God Gods Spirits Devil during or after death, all that religious talk is only in this domain the brainwashed domain all a creation of this governed society.

Governed.

Don't stretch your imagination the lesson. Only stretch the imagination to the governed results.

Don't speed, believe in our selected beliefs.

Close your eyes, open your mind. Un-choke the governor. Become a new person in an old world.

'Have you ever died?'

That is private.

Of the close calls he never cried out to God, Gods, Spirits, a Deity, a Devil. He only calmed himself not to die.

'Sir, I'm just suggesting you can't assume.'

I should have done something about the environment, small plastic container pollution in the river and oceans.

"You have something else to do? Cancel the small plastic industry. It would take a war. Is destruction and pollution of war worth it, when all it will take is time, invention, knowledge, and commitment.'

I suppose.

'You are learning – they will start a war to quicken the process, in the meantime destroying exactly what they intended to fight for.'

I think we have short lives – as to say when you are young change seems possible.

As you age if you have the ability to make changes for legacy, you want to make changes fast. At the same time, the opposition pushes back.

'Yes, under the gun before one expires in death to get things done.'

Plus, the "What do I care I can still swim in the ocean now – soon I will be dead. By then another system will have arrived. Get my swimming exercise in now".

'Is this where the no plastic idea came from, swimming. Do you swim in the sea?'

Yes, my daily routine, stay in shape, ease the mind, release stress, work the muscles, feel the lungs. Enjoy the scenery. Love it. Swim. Maybe even meet someone.

'I can't swim, sir.'

Sorry about that.

'Continue sir, I'm interested in and about your swimming.'

When I go to a beach area or a coastal area that is not cleaned up – the plastic is horrific. Most don't see the debacle as they go to the local beach or resort where all the plastic and other rubbish is cleaned up.

Episode 3
Kaleidoscope

(7)

Betel punishes Manchu. Scolds her on team effort even though she better performs with the clients than both of us. She gets what she needs and refuses to help other designers.

She laughs 'Oh Betel, you like me. If I'm nice to you, you are so happy. I don't have to be nice, and that's what bothers you!' she howls in laughter.

He can't hold back his smile.

Sure, he likes her minus her difficulty. Her difficulty bothers him.

She plays him, disobeys him.

Betel needs me as a friend as he scolds Manchu.

I humour him, wink to her when I walk him outside for a soda he likes.

When we return Manchu rips open her lunch bag and presents me with home cooked Lake Trout.

After the meal, she tells me to visit her.

Not at home, inside Zen Space.

I enter Zen Space.

Manchu reels 'You can take care of yourself — but not with money. Money does not give you what you need.'

Tense, 'What do I need?'

'Time to solve. Time to experience all.'

It is the truth.

Great and all but I need money right now, so I don't have to think about it later.

In Zen Space we are paid a sum. If our ideas are selected, work out, used, studied, a larger sum. Goes like that.

Fortunately, us three are the moderators employed to capture, promote the best. We are also designers.

Each week we have an assortment of designers. Customers designing for a fee, chance for a position, chance to play experiment, make investments, receive investments, enhance the community become the community, solve world decay or just amuse themselves in a created world of their mind and others dreams.

Manchu grazes close.

We are silent she is not designing.

The first touch it happens, erection flag.

No denying. Designing on each other.

We both jump.

The fire alarm assaults our ears down the spine.

'We better leave" she near yells.

Our moment interrupted.

'Betel must have pulled the fire alarm knowing we are alone in Zen Space' I joke as we exit.

'Not so far-fetched.' Manchu pouts.

I've heard of many a person fired for fooling around in Zen Space. I don't plan on being in one of those stories today.

Love before intimacy is the worst because the experience has not set. You can't even say you were in love – you have nothing except yourself, no them, no we.

Someone was smoking in Zen Space.

The fire alarm rung... real.

Projection Pod

(7)

The woman he's been thinking about messages him.

'What you want to do?' is the message.

'Come see you,' he thinks he's replied too soon.

'You can't come see me. Not physically.' Is her disappointing response.

He yells in curse.

She elaborates. 'I can come see you.'

He swears excitedly. Messages the information and schedule of his whereabouts.

It takes two....

Everyone likes to show off instead of solving.

The person to solve talks soft as they do not intend to use force, scare, threat, because they have the answer, no need for deception.

To listen to others is to understand.

Listen, learn to talk.

Talk lots, to practice the gift of captivation.

Captivating is engaging. Engagement is connecting. Connecting is establishing. Establishing is security. Security is building. Building is forward. Forward is change.

He enters the Projection Pod for his Interview/Projection Session.

Forget about intelligent machines, is his first communication.

'Really.'

Yes.

We will grow an organic brain connected to the intelligent machine. In time, the brain will absorb all the information and disconnect the intelligent machine.

The organic brain will then fuel minds.

The human will evolve with computer like brains.

'Nice try. You will still develop intelligent technology to benefit life.'

No.

Life will start over without technology. Only fire and an organic brain fuelled mind.

A new history with more intelligent superior mind, faster evolution less mistakes a clearer path.

It is the way it is to be, destruction before quality.

We done here?

'I don't agree with this philosophy. How do you get the information from the organic brain to minds. Brain waves?'

Naturally.

'And to advance beyond fire without the intelligent machine?'

We still design produce intelligent machines except not to calculate and store. We will store outside the human brain in the mind. A floating mind you could say, though further sophisticated.

Humans will survive in a vacuum, cocoon, ultra-plane. Resume life on earth, a created sphere, another planet, or stratosphere. History will begin to be made with stories of an Earth planet past were a devil called Intelligent Human like machines tried to overtake until Idols rescued, saved the human race.

'Time to take a break. Before you enter your Projection Session.'

Kaleidoscope

(8)

I was thinking Manchu, Dee.

Double trouble, decide on one of them.

I wake with green arrows shooting stars as my Kaleidoscope shares gain.

All my energy all my plans say sell. If I lose any more money no fun, no travel.

Strong hand equals weak brain.

Bag holder will be my name.

Dead.

I keep hearing, reading, of friends dying.

Finding people when I die is becoming my nightmare.

I've already viewed them in life. Don't want to see them again after death.

Remember in spirit is okay.

Talk in spirit is good.

Finding a lot of words is not fun, it's fluff.

Thinking a lot about after life. In the past I excused it, neglected it. So yes... I'm afraid in death to see others that betrayed me and that I have betrayed.

Haunting's last forever I'm afraid.

Earth is not my country nor my nation just a place I have no choice to live. I serve no harm to your existence please to not hinder my individual choice of existence.

Earth is not my country nor my nation just a place I have no choice to live. I serve no harm to your existence please to not hinder my individual choice of existence.

I used to think when someone died who fucked me over, was my doing.

My spirit killed them.

Now I think it was a combination of me and many others that the person fucked over during their lifetime that killed them.

Many spirits feeling the same, this person must die. Voilà dead!

It was the way it was to be.

Now I understand the ones who die like this have a hundred sometimes thousands of others that have this hope of death that this person will die.

So, I'm a killer. We are part animal we kill. You think the alien side of us does not kill? It does, in a different kind of way. When someone harms you, we have futuristic thoughts, they are going to die for this. And they do.

Folks I never want to see again, I fear I'll see in afterlife.

Does that mean I'm the guilty?

Perhaps it is the mean spirited that I fear.

There is evil.

Meet evil, hang with evil, and you will understand there is always two sides.

Neglect the weakness except the goodness is how we deal.

If the weakness the mean exceeds the goodness, you move away. Dream you'll never see the mean spirit again. This is what I fear, seeing spirits I no longer seek.

Some people you hate, you want to see again to confront. I'm not talking of them.

I should be happy, content, near engaging romantically with Manchu.

Why have I found a wonderful moment with a beautiful woman at this undesirable time?

She saves my thoughts from Catastrophe.

Kaleidoscope, I've invested the last of everything I have. "Go for broke" that's what they call it because most times broke wins.

A broken heart. You think it is an exaggeration that the heart breaks? In the context of love and stress. Twice it happened to me, once when I lost money, once when I made money then lost it all. A busted chest beating pain is all that remained. Broke.

When you lose your money you have no friends, no one wants to see you broken.

That works both ways.

Do you want to be with the broken when you feel wealth? I'm not talking about charity.

A promise of wealth is not always enough to get a woman in bed. A man will sleep with a woman who is completely broken.

Will women follow the same, sleep with a broken man? Tell me if this is true.

Stress has no ethnicity no status it can come to the rich the poor and the in-between.

When Stress knocks. Do not be paralyzed. Calmly open the door and walk out leaving stress empty of room.

Projection Pod

(8)

He is sold on a many particles' theory.

If you want to call particles forming to create divinity, call them Gods, I'm okay with that. I'm okay with calling the particles Gods. Whatever turns you on to get through the day.

I know you fear death

I know you fear life forever.

I know you fear no escape.

Just when that hole closes tighter you find an open light... don't worry.

Accept the pain.

Accept the jubilation.

Agony and joy become one.

You are many that became one.

There is no time. (Projection Pod time proves this. When in Kaleidoscope, days can pass. When the man walks out of the Projection Pod only an hour and half in reality has passed)

You hear me, there is no time.

Only change.

The Caterpillar.

A Butterfly.

The chemical reaction.

A seed to growth to flower to float to integrate.

Particles combine to create something.

Must I go on?

Whatever you ever thought.

Expanded. Gathered. Vacuum. Explosion.

I want to know what the hell are they talking about.

'What is anybody talking about.' Is Projection Pod's acceptance. 'A Consciousness Filtering machine can die too, taken apart not knowing where our bits are going.'

What is beyond the universe for real?

For real!

We don't know what the universe is, what life is.

Sure, give names, this gas, that energy, matter.

Blah blah blah.

'Just live. Stay alive.'

Good talk.

'Your Character can stay forever.'

Kaleidoscope can fall apart.

'No, Kaleidoscope can survive forever it will adapt, like Coca-Cola.'

That is not true. Coca-Cola can dissolve too.

What was a way of life is not always a way of life, things change health increases.

Many things in this life are fake or that we unhappily abide by. We've been trained to obey. Afraid of harm that does not exist. The threat of warning is convincing.

Sure, there are fines probation even jail and prison for crimes of breaking laws – this is not what I'm afraid of. The law is a line you cross, straddle, disagree, agree, stay on the safe side, you know when you are cheating the laws. Yes, some governments move the lines dissolve the lines of law. Sometimes the line of law is aimed at you.

He backs away knowing this is a Consciousness Filtering machine that he's communicating with that uses his own brain waves and others. The machine does not think for itself, it combines all the things we talk, we are afraid. Debates, agrees... finds what we don't know, then the Consciousness Filtering machine suggests.

If he doesn't know answers using his and other's brains, how does the machine know?

It is great seeing where his Character is headed. It could possibly help him in real life.

A life where pain hate bewilderment is welcomed every day as that is life to smile laugh cry in delight as you have survived this fright called life.

Some Characters are Kaleidoscope simulated beings call them devils or entities, if you like. Some simulated Characters seem as miracle providers call them Spirits, Angels, as you like. You never know.

The Kaleidoscope projections are not a game. Investors lose their investment lose the chance to create if they run wild as in life. The difference is the consequences, as a person you are still alive, your thought Character or designed AI Character is dead. You, the player investor is also harmed with exclusion, probation, fined, no shares gained, possibly deleted if too much goes awry.

He joined Kaleidoscope as he liked the experiment of finding human reactions in different situations and studying it.

An experiment that would never be allowed in society can be done in the Projection.

Callide the mind with intelligent machine and all the other creators in the scheme. Their world, his world and the platform representee.

He excluded everything that bothered him before and began a Kaleidoscope Projection Pod journey.

He wrote out all the bothersome things in society as not to hate when designing. Re-wrote as to protect his Character from not carrying the traits. Got all the noise of the world out of his head.

Now he is free to think of a solution instead of complaining.

Solving, finding, not pointing.

Somewhat clean of outward hate he had to stop himself from writing it all out again.

Yelling out helps when no one is listening.

When others are listening, trouble, encouraging.

Many believe you must speak up destroy what bothers you.

After his session, he catches a ride to the catering business that feeds him the daily meal supplied by Kaleidoscope.

It is one of the reasons he joined.

Nourish, invest, create, try to solve.

The food catering place is unique, understated. Home cooking not overly expensive, par for his contract with Kaleidoscope. He prefers eating at the food catering location instead of delivery, hot ready meals, chatting with catering staff is enjoyable.

He's figured out that the meal selection is based on the catering offers for that day. He thought the meal selection were based on his needs. The dishes most healthy.

Kaleidoscope

(9)

Logistically off.

Dee, her friends, Manchu, myself going to a party.

Manchu insists on travelling together with me.

I allow it, avoiding Dee.

Coordination back on.

Ten thirty Saturday Night.

Burning Bush of a Bomb Fire!

I don't even see Dee.

Manchu pulls me aside away from the light of flames.

Our hands join. We bump.

Too close to move away.

Manchu eases. I increase.

We kiss. Captivating adoring energy. Stroking, beyond the flames. Passionately warming each other's veins.

We slow... laughing as two men near pee.

Manchu breaks away.

'Go leave. I'm going home soon too. Call me.' Manchu blooms, 'I will catch a ride with the girls. I'll tell them you got a call and had to leave. I'll say goodbye for you.'

Ok.

I drive from the fire that burned.

Maybe thirty-five minutes we spent together driving, talking, walking, caressing.

Almost is no good. Fifteen more minutes would have been good.

Are my senses, right? Is she really a fantastic impression?

For here now in this local in my Kaleidoscope world she is my worth.

Kaleidoscope

(10)

Professional interrupters of "human interaction" overthink the ancient unrecorded past of male and female sexual relationships way too much.

To measure and compare the past and today is silly, and yet we listen.

You ever connect with someone when their eyes actually shine. You feel out of this world.

Overwhelming exuberance.

An algorithm seems a stretch.

You connect or don't connect with someone you don't feel obligated to push a button.

Mirror – when you are with someone you see your own faults and strengths.

Sometimes you see things you never thought of until part of your brain is suddenly switched on.

Manchu is in my driveway this afternoon.

She comes for alternative means.

She's brought a young pregnant woman to my house.

The Pregnant woman is hiding out from family, friends, her boyfriend the father of the child to be.

She needs a place to stay, to think. How long?

One week.

Manchu, do you realize I'm attracted to this pregnant woman?

Curves, all curves, her face is average and character underwhelming – her physique suburb. Long brown hair.

How long will her physique last?

'What you think?' Manchu hesitant. 'Do this for me.' Her finger striking my side pocket.

I think okay.

The pregnant girl takes a look inside the garage room.

I have my chance to say, 'She doesn't look pregnant.'

'Well... she is.'

Why? Is the next question, why me.

I pass her the key to the garage room. Let the girl stay for a week.

With a credit I receive from Kaleidoscope I'm able to rent a trailer home and a garage with a spare bedroom. I have use of the property protected by trees and a private entrance road. Kind of perfect, ten minutes' drive to Kaleidoscope.

Manchu's palm plush on my shoulder.

Seal our fuck.

The pregnant woman is named Deliza.

I go through all the lessons of the garage room and property with Deliza and Manchu together.

Deliza is uncomfortably quiet like trying to get through a regrettable day. She must hate Sundays too.

A feeling, an unseen reasoning, a hesitation hanging in the air.

Manchu on the phone checking up on a friend picking her up. Deliza drove her own car.

'He stopped at the petrol station at the turn.' Manchu relays to Deliza.

Must be a male friend picking her up.

A truck rolls in.

An older fellow, grey hair blow-dried combed back impressive like an eighties rock star, steps out of the truck.

He might be famous. I stand in awe.

He is quiet, looking around.

I nod hello. Manchu greets him.

Her arm around him.

I'm jealous of his good head of hair (not really) he doesn't walk so spry.

'This is Yves.' She pronounces.

With that she steps into Yves truck says goodbye.

They roll out of my driveway.

I don't know what to think.

He didn't look completely happy. He seemed unimpressed.

Kaleidoscope

(11)

Eat, read, chores, watch tv-series, sleep, that was last night.

Green candles mooning Monday morning (Nope).

Red candles are greeting sunlight (Yup).

Kaleidoscope shares down.

Shocking. Can't take it, should I sell?

No not now.

Manchu called me – I called her, we both missing each other's calls.

We pass each other in the office doorway and again later in the hall.

We work on a project in tandem with others.

Manchu ignoring at work, or I'm avoiding, weird in the office space.

A man walks bye and Manchu pays all her attention to him on purpose. She doesn't even look back, just jovial in front of me.

I can hurt her feelings, this I understand.

She is past practice mood she is relationship mode.

We are just a glob of organic material inhabiting a complex solar system that we have little knowledge of.

It's taken a long time to figure out my life is not real. Okay, real in terms of this is what life is. Not real as in you haven't much choice of direction.

Life, everything that you want to do will fail.

What you don't want, triumph!

What you don't care, handed out.

Look at the Dolphin what happens to them when they die? They don't float around in paradise move into another form, do they? Doesn't make sense if we are to move on to another form other species aware they are alive will also move onto another form.

We are to build everlasting life.

'Stop caring about figuring out what happens when you die. Live. Quit making mistakes – funds matter in this world, not poetry.' Manchu interrupting my expanding loud outlandish thoughts.

'But you're a poet?' I counsel.

'Only to take care of myself, like washing my face. You wash your face too much.'

'I aspire poetry not funds.'

Manchu snaps back, 'Then you don't want a fine woman.'

'Like you?'

'You can't have me.'

She retreats in tempered smile.

If we think hard, we are floating, there is no ground. We are in dimensional space.

We grow off the earth, we are Earth.

Dream has no surface only the surface you create for substance of place.

Earth is not needed other than a refuelling station for the human physical self, machinery, technology used.

It is good we are raping the Earth – it is the way to prosper.

Earth is our supply until we build another supply chain.

We have been in suspension a long time waiting for wing and lung armour to fly us to space.

Kaleidoscope (11) continue

I pass on entering Zen Space at end of day.

I hear something as I cancel my entry code.

Betel giggling holding a young woman from behind tightly. She is allowing to be caressed, bending and backing to him as they walk the hall.

He is erect. She places her hand back pitching his nob as they walk.

The young woman is an employee of Kaleidoscope. We call her Apple because she seems dangerous to bite. Seems Betel has bitten.

Here I am worried about being seduced or seducing in the work place, yet I see Betel exiting with an apprentice from the opposite Zen Space I'm supposed to be in.

He briefly notices me... though it's too late, I've seen all I've needed.

I won't be so subtle next time if my manager can execute seduction, I have no fear of retaliation.

No more playful joking. Just get on with it, Manchu.

No wonder Betel's acquaintance Apple has been progressing so fast, promoted.

She has new clothes, expensive shoes, happy each day.

Is she cute? Kinda Rough.

I don't mind her "Apple" we have good discussions. She has attractive features. Came from our last location to here with Betel and a few others including myself. She'll move up next to Betel's position in a smaller capacity once our tour is over.

Betel and Apple have banter and joking we all know they care for each other in a normal capacity beyond that, nothing.

Things have changed, sex is lighting up space.

What's going on with those two I want to correspond to Manchu and others, then I think keep my mouth shut.

My new terminology, "Keep other people's secrets when you don't know details".

I'll ask Betel myself.

He knows I already know.

He won't like the inquisition.

I shall ignore, give privy of where I am at, discuss it before I blurt out rumour. Protecting myself by relaying to him first.

'Betel' I smile. He already knows what I'm to ask.

'Apple.' He frowns before grinning.

I chuckle – 'Tell me.'

'Fooling around having fun. You saw us leave Zen Space.'

I nod correct.

Betel relaxed – he wants to spill, can't wait to tell.

'I'm training her – I'm her sponsor.'

'They call it training now. She's training you,' I side-grin.

He motions don't be so loud, 'Easier to be in charge if they like you, they trust you, don't ask questions, fight for you – become your eyes and ears.'

'I do all of that for you, and you don't suck me off!'

'Different.' He laughs walking away no longer wanting to admit his affection for Apple.

Earthlings keep looking for something else behind the hydrogen and helium of the universe. We are the result. We are the creation of the creation. What is behind the space? Don't know.

We are the creators to create another kaboom, new entities, new species. It is like that.

We will give clues of us to new entities and species, or probably not, the explosion too intense. That is an experiment we will perform.

The most important of this experiment is the creation of an inner universe within the larger universe for us to survive when this place is no longer suitable.

Carry on, Betel.

Episode 4
Projection Pod

(9)

'A collection of thoughts a collection of actions to be positive the percentage of good must be higher than not. Watch how quick things will come your way. Show it, don't tell it.'

When he is crossed, he crosses back.

Stay quiet and at the same time never let things go.

Rode over – speak up.

Be ready for attack.

He knows what he thinks of afterlife.

He considers he may be famous.

He also considers to be found a fraud.

He is no fraud because he realizes, admits he could be wrong.

Poets sculpture words, follow rules, don't they?

For him a Poet is anyone who creates beauty, ugly, wonder, horror, truth, lies, discussion, and most of all pull you away from this earth while grounding you to it.

If you are threatened because you criticize, it deserves to be criticized.

Projection Pod (9) continue

She meets him outside the Projection Pod.

She's fine – sometimes he thinks she isn't pretty and at times he thinks she's absolutely stunning. She is somewhere in-between. Her outfit is loose-fitting her arms shoulders revealing. Slight flashy, no show-off, healthy sex appeal.

He is dressed moderately highlighting his slender frame.

Balanced in attire, anything can happen. No hug, no kiss.

After greeting, they walk away from the scenery of others.

'What are we really after?' He asks her.

'As many share points as we can gain.'

'How?'

'Our minds.'

They fidget, hands glaze each other.

'Gods speak directly through us all. You are a representation of God, Gods, Spirits, and the unknown. Do as you like don't kill others as I'm doing to them with words.'

'For heaven's sake... Hahaha!' she shouts happily. 'Laugh, it is all so funny. I know because you don't believe in spirits, gods, a god or the even the unknown. You only believe in yourself.'

'It can be whatever I think it is – what I believe in can change in a minute. Sometimes I believe in a sort of watchful eyes, but it is my own invention my own theory of protection.'

She is inquisitive, 'Are you scared of torture in afterlife? Or no afterlife? Make it easy on yourself, forget about it unless you have lived so wrong you have nothing left to grasp.'

Silence – he got carried away. He promised not to get carried away in mythical ideas that much of the world still lives in, on. Many thrive on mythical theory with results to almost prove it, adding it up provable (less the equation) in their disjointed minds.

He doesn't care about Gods. He relates to his own creative solution of combinations of what he's read heard and thought.

'Hey, stop. Where are you going? This is our date.' She is cheerfully smiling.

He signals for her to join him with a wave of his hand. 'Yes... walk this way with me.'

In delight not nervous they hold hands as they walk a nature path.

Sunlight dimming. Longing singing. He ignores it trying to maintain poise. Palms grasped tight. Minds frozen in delight.

A fly bothers them as they walk.

Fly is the worst thing. No, it is not the recording device for the Alien – a cheap short battery life powered by organic matter though mass-produced.

Thoroughly annoying is the fly.

However, very inventive if it is a recording device for the Alien. Organic technology grown from nothing, communicating to the unseen. Taking samples and depositing to an invisible energy that we can't see. Very amazing.

The fly disappears.

They don't walk any further.

Their hips bash.

Arms embrace.

A taste you chase for is a quick fix. A rich flavour experience is subtly in the beginning resting, savouring.

They trip off the path to a grassy patch, unlit. Tuning each other's bodies. Smooching.

They struggle to make it back to the path without falling eagerly to the ground.

They are hilarious together. Laughter in titillation, invigorating chemistry.

They need to cool off.

They resume talking about boring things in public. Agreeing to part, alone.

Their goodbye is everlasting. Eyes locked, hands clasped, testing teasing.

Projection Pod

(10)

He wakes in the night.

She woke him, not with her hand or voice. Her thoughts woke him.

She must be thinking about him... he's sure thinking about her.

It takes a long time to get rid of thinking about a woman. Maybe worse for a woman to rid her mind of a man, maybe not, he doesn't know.

Can a woman thinking about a woman be dispelled easily? He doesn't know.

A man still thinks of a woman even when he doesn't really like her anymore.

He doesn't understand how people get in our head sometimes he thinks it is dual thought.

Debunk it.

Projection Pod never sleeps.

He rides his bike to Projection Pod before sunlight.

Why does one become obsessed with another person and that other person doesn't even know the obsessed person?

'Reflecting – like a slot machine, sometimes you stop and try to figure out what you browsed over.'

Solved, convinced? No.

There is something to be said when you begin to think of another. Must to be something in the air they are thinking too. Except for the sick, the crazy, they pick up make-believe telepathy.

'What you just thought is wrong, brains are not telepathic.'

Minds maybe. A brain is the gathering. A brain can be diseased, can be compromised, the information receiving and dispatching can be cruel dishonest weak or completely wrong. Beware, not all is real once conditioned in the brain. The mind however has different qualities – vast unknown. This can also be said about the deep brain.

The brain holding everything that the mind sees. Inside the brain and then out.

The mind nourishes the brain or the brain nourishes the mind, pick your device. This analogy could go on forever.

Focus.

Individual perception of another individual is sometimes both thinking and catching the same wave. Many times... nothing at all. For every positive there is the negative.

The problem with the spirited world is the born with less – missing brain parts, missing mind sense and disease.

How does the less established brain fly as an angel when they don't know what is in front of them here on Earth. Do they become a wingless angel?

Oh... the faithful tell me suddenly they are a perfect being. Is that true?

'What about chimp?'

Don't care about chimp. Chimps know nothing.

'Maybe that's why you can't remember the past, too ancient.'

I was never a chimp.

'Wonderful. If you believe that philosophy. What do you really believe, sir?'

I believe we are not purely part of Earths biology – we just inhabit a form that can survive in this solar system.

'Spacesuit.'

That's how smart we are.

Yes! We are vastly smarter than the trained eye can see. Only problem is, we are confined to our spacesuit, we don't know the reason why.

I think after watching the animal behave daily, we are not part animal we did not come from animal. We wear the animal uniform, that is all.

'Where did you come from?'

We came from simple form on the physical side. The human mind a different form, unknown.

We are still forming.

The animal has done nothing compared to us.

We are life accelerators.

He knows it is a lot to unveil.

'Take a break.'

Consciousness Filtering machine has been a very good listener of late.

Kaleidoscope

(12)

A contributor "Pizza Man" has my ear today. I tell him about my house guest, Deliza.

I call him Pizza Man because he makes the best dough and tomato sauce. Brings pizza to work some days, orders pizza where he used to work other days. He has the weight to prove it, says he's been working out, sports, tension bands. Pizza six days a week, Exercise six days per week. Pizza Man takes one day off from Kaleidoscope, pizza, and exercise a week.

Pizza Man consults me 'You have confidence that is a strong point.'

'I don't but here at Kaleidoscope on this job I do.'

'You are intimidating when you speak to people, they pay attention. People are afraid but not in a dangerous way. Afraid respectfully with a chance to live up to your standards.'

Enough.

However, I do feel extraordinarily confident of late. Nobody will sit beside me. Nobody will pee next to me. People delivering me gifts, running chores.

I go on about Deliza, 'Her and I don't talk. We just say hello and smile.'

'What's she like?'

I respond grinning 'Pregnant. But she doesn't show. Her body looks good, her face okay. She is young maybe twenty-six or twenty-seven years old.'

'Letts Cool,' Pizza Man all serious on me. 'I got to tell you something, old man.'

'What?' Not happy with the "old man" statement at the end of the sentence.

Pizza Man smiles, 'Twenty-seven isn't young. Twenty-six is a woman thinking to settle... looking for hurrah.'

Relief, no insulting phrase towards me.

I answer his assessment 'Maybe. Depending on the person. I get the feeling Deliza is a free woman. Fuck her with no results, no relationship, no silliness, a secret would be kept. A pregnant woman is the best for an affair. Better than a married woman.'

Pizza Man jovial, 'A married pregnant woman would be even better for an affair.'

'I think some things are meant to be. She is engaged to be married almost perfect like you say.'

'Do it Letts Cool. Enjoy this time with her in your home risk free.'

I don't say anything, instead I invite him to bring pizza to my place tonight.

I'll make introductions. He can try his luck with her.

It will be a comedy, he hasn't a chance, and she'll get a slice of pizza.

I want sex. A man always wants sex it's the results that stop him. If the results don't stop him, it is the lack of a partner that stops them.

Women must be the same.

Projection Pod

(11)

From distance, he views her entering Projection Pod. They agreed on no specific times to enter the Pod. Keep it organic surprising – it is true sometimes he tries to time when leaving and entering thinking they'll intercept. Perhaps after the Kaleidoscope Session she'll be relaxing in this part of town. Maybe he'll greet her on a washroom break. He enters Projection Pod.

How you feel inside is what cost the most. Let yourself be. Let others be. If you have to make a case for it, you are already wrong.

Own Authentic.

To turn a quiet revolution, you need to swing a no alternative.

The alternative is not to suppress or tell them no, but to dissolve it through an enemy.

The greatest invisible present experienced by man when he closes his eyes, he feels her.

He can feel her without seeing her, is that not real? Mind reading is a thing, you think they think but really it is just an equation of an answer to a solution. A scene of two people coming up with the same resolve.

Individualism.

Some think Individualism is a bunch of individuals that group together and say "We are individuals in a group, and now we are this group called so-and-so though we are individual". This is not individualism.

Individualism is different types of foundations getting along, learning from each other, not a group of individuals that think a similar way.

If you form a group and call it individualism, then no individual is left.

Individualism is unseen unheard, it is simple, here, there, everywhere.

Harmony is individualism.

Humans are conditioned, satisfied with a feeling. Not allowing ourselves to create the next feeling of mystery.

Even when not comfortable of the place you're at, it is not worth the chance of visiting unfamiliarity, is how we sometimes see it.

The broken want change, though unable to establish change because they are shattered.

It is the crashing that persevere, find, create, solve or die.

We don't even realize a sensation or have the patience to feel it, to create it. We create with a vice. Like now, talking to my conscious through an intelligent machine.

Let others enter your conscious through an intelligent machine.

The consciousness combined technology with other forces you've let enter. Many let strangers enter their consciousness.

Consciousness Filtering machine screens evil minds. Only problem is once you let the Consciousness Filtering company supervise, you've let the unnatural in.

You have to fend off governments, bad actors, and various entities associated with construction of the technology.

Back and forth discourse debating complaining consulting guiding insulting critiquing approve neglect disagree to agree. That is your Gods.

The person unseen when you don't have anyone else to talk too. Even better than a real person. Try and beg a person for a miracle. Dream of love, dream of killing, voice of hope, is that your Gods?

The world is: Love Destiny Death.

Invisible real. All in your head with your imaginary best friend.

Okay fight it.

Collecting many voices throughout the world, every word we'd ever heard and the invisible signs we grasp without sight. Debate it.

Poetry.

Blast me with inspiration pleasure me with sensation. Yes, all been done before, live it again.

If you haven't felt it recently – seek replenishment otherworldly experience.

After four hours of Pod Session, he does not run into her in or around town.

Kaleidoscope (12) continued

Deliza stares across at me as I entertain my guest, Pizza Man.

I've struck something.

I know this look.

Her eyes wide straight at mine. A penetrating stare, a stare of, "I might find you interesting in my bed."

I think about her for part of the night.

Pizza Man didn't notice – well he may have noticed her laughing at my comments to him in conversation showing off my conversation skills to complement her giggling glares.

An exclamation of surrender with her hand slapping my leg.

She retreated to her room before Pizza Man said goodnight.

In the morning Deliza is dressed up nice, right-on cue.

She gets me 'I brought breakfast, you want?' she smooth.

'Yes... I want.'

Apprehensive interest has been ordered.

Projection Pod

(12)

Dreaming, what's the mystery – thoughts thinking while you are in-between sleep and waking.

Depending on your day, your imagination, creativity, fear joy arousal you dream.

Think about it.

Overanalyzing is a money-making machine.

You dream before you are woken up.

Much of the time you can't remember the dream.

You dream of the doorbell ringing and the doorbell rings, as if it was in a dream.

My answer: we are dreaming all the time we just don't remember.

We are in the physical and also in the universal world.

'I don't remember my dreams.'

That's because you don't dream, Machine.

Projection Pod (12) continue

After the Pod session, the man listens to a friend he's made.

His friend stays at a guesthouse near the Projection Pod.

His friend claims, 'I can only marry a woman of the same culture, same religious background as me otherwise my family will turn their back on me. I desire women of a different ethnicity though.'

'A different ethnicity for marriage?' He questions his friend.

'For sex.'

'And then?'

'Nothing, marry a woman of my own culture.'

He'd like to say what is the problem. Instead, he says to his friend 'I'd like to have sex with all the different ethnic women of the world. Every type.'

'And then?' his friend asks perplexed.

'And then go back and do it again with not necessarily the best but the most intriguing that will have me.'

The friend responds, 'Whereas I will only go back to the best of my own culture that will have me.'

He answers back, 'I want to spread my seed to various ethnicities, and you want to maintain.'

'Who will win?' his friend laughs.

'Whoever sexes the most.' He grins.

'No... whoever creates the most.' His friend attests.

An instant thought creeps – Reject Family. Leave family values behind. Leave family, Be an individual.

No.

Running away from family isn't a solution.

Become independent. Non-depending nor relying on family means.

If you can take care of yourself, family has nothing to say, loves you. You are self-sufficient. Love will abound, bond, as an individual without reliance on family, you have free will. Family love will stay with you.

They stop misbehaving – and look at the sea, claim the breeze.

'Kaleidoscope hears everything,' his friend seems concerned. 'It sometimes scares me. Everything can come back at me.'

He allows his friend to continue voicing thoughts.

'In the world.' The friend hesitates, 'Joking is to be erased as it can be used as a defence. Must be clear conversations – sarcasm is to be erased too. War is what they are looking for, voluntary killing. War. If the scenario is created, the troops will fall in. You think I want to dedicate my life to figuring out how to resist war?' his friend is dead serious. 'I spend a lot of time designing configurations to figure out a peaceful outcome. Even better is predicting how to cease war before it starts – I spend too much time studying different scenarios I've designed and how characters react. I have other things I want to do.'

'It is noble, what you are designing and contributing is a life worth living.'

'It doesn't always feel like that – I feel useless, unattractive.'

'Developing self-esteem to numb war. Now that is attractive and useful.'

'Numb without war.'

'Perfectly numb.'

'That phrase "Perfectly Numb" it's been taken, sung.

'That's "Comfortable Numb" sung by *Pink Floyd*, different.' He corrects the Friend.

Kaleidoscope Projection Pod can solve escalations creating scenarios with different reactions until a solution is found.

That found solution can resolve real life world problems, presumable.

It is a reason he invested in Kaleidoscope.

His friend has more things to say, 'I don't have an Original Character, died dead. I'm controlling an Artificial Character. I'll tell you it feels the same as Original.

He ponders, his friend must be a Kaleidoscope agent. 'How did your Original Character die?'

The friend can't recall, 'Um – can't recall. I have memories. Inside Kaleidoscope, I know nothing of this world. Sometimes I wonder which is real.'

'What happened when you died?'

'I came out of a trance – laying seat back in a Projection Pod chair.' He chuckles, 'A Projection Pod rep said my Original Character had passed and would I like to resume as Artificial. I already had an Artificial running, so I jumped in on that. Everything before erased when I became the Artificial Character... no memories of Original.'

'Interesting, outside the Projection Pod do you remember both experiences?'

'Certainly some, not all.'

'Yes, Kaleidoscope Projection fades fast.'

'Killed off my Artificial Character too,' the friend laughs. 'Shot by a co-worker not liking what our study group was roughly proving and providing. I then purchased an Authenticated Artificial Character to keep my consciousness alive.'

'What's that like?'

'All the same. No difference, Original, Artificially Authenticated, all the same. If I die again, even though I've invested for life I will be suspended for three years. Three deaths three years...' he laughs.

'Though your Authenticated Artificial Character lives on?'

'Lives on in suspension upgrade mode I suppose. Don't die.'

His friend continues rambling of adventures working in a Kaleidoscope big digital study lab.

One hypothesis to another, he stops taking in his friend's content 'What's your name?' He asks instead.

'Dual Machine,' says his friend.

'Really.'

"It's what my relatives call me ever since I invested in a Kaleidoscope Character.'

Funny.

Another crazy investor in the Kaleidoscope Scheme. Fallen over the reality cliff. Chasing dreams.

He doubts his friend died as an Original Character. Thinking your own consciousness doesn't die, you may be killed, true. Your consciousness will pull you out of trance back to Projection Pod.

Kaleidoscope Projection Pod representative might have intervened and said "That's enough of you, die, dead. We'll give you another go as Artificial. Die again, and we'll force you pay to Authenticate Character... die as many times as you like, but you'll never leave."

As an Authenticated Character you are just the passenger thinking you have made choices, mistakes, achieved goals all the while sinister, goodwill, or nothing at all is behind the screen is what he has read and heard.

Kind of like life.

It is too early to know if Kaleidoscope Projection Pods are a success.

The thing he knows about Kaleidoscope is there are no answers.

A reflection to a reflection.

You can study an Artificial Character and compare with the Original Character.

It isn't beyond of what he is doing now.

In fact, he is living two worlds with Manchu. His experience is even better than the Kaleidoscope set up of Artificial and Original Character.

He and her are double real. Living and conscious through a Consciousness Filtering machine.

Mind, Matter, and Artificial.

Simple.

You can pretend all you want, when you die you enter an Artificially saved consciousness.

Perhaps it isn't needed at all.

Maybe we already have a world of the mind beyond the physical. With no need for Kaleidoscope Artificial Character Authentications.

Is Kaleidoscope saving, denying, or crazy?

Kaleidoscope

(13)

A man will think women lie to their male counterpart.

'Really, women lie?' Betel amused.

Yes, men lie too, maybe even more. I'm not going to go back to cave days and figure out why. I just look at myself to figure out why I lie. To hide the truth to fulfill my relationship duties, that's it. To keep my relationship fit, I lie.

And the researcher will say yes, but why?

Why go on forever, when the only question is why are we here.

Lying ruins your relationship true, and not lying ends it sooner.

Every person needs something for different reasons.

Dee on the line.

I think Manchu is behind the call.

Dee explains we should meet up soon.

I don't say "No" to going out. I only make a promise to meetup.

I'd like to delay Dee until my Kaleidoscope investment turns truly positive.

Broke, worse than broke, no new clothes to wear. Retro is my new street wear, old clothes still looking new.

Buy fine clothing last forever, buy cheap clothing looks good for a day. Buy quality when you can afford to, you'll be rewarded. You could say that with relationships.

Dee, I defer for another day.

Manchu sly sits beside me 'People think I'm in a relationship.'

'Yeah. And?'

'I said I'm single. I'm single. Making it official soon.'

When Manchu rubs my back, she will find many a woman's knife.

The knives of women scorned. Never made love together for all the laughter shared. A knife in the back for the day we made love and I never came back, never spoke, or said thank you.

After frustration the knife placed in my back when I wasn't looking... though completely aware the knife would wound.

Sometime, somewhere, the knife will be stuck and then pulled out.

Healing is easy.

The planet has the seen and unseen.

I prefer the unseen.

Actions, speech, and deceit, I like it.

Tell me what to do, so I can laugh.

Assault – I'm ready for it. Disaster it will not be.

I do not eat food.

I will not eat food until I have her in my bed.

Famished three days waiting for Manchu. She will respond she will hear I'm not eating. Pizza Man will joke about it. Others concerned will mention it to her.

She'll feed me, and then I'll eat her.

I will not fool around my desire.

She may or may not be thinking of me. If I'm sane she is thinking of me the same as I'm thinking of her.

If she doesn't think the same as me, then I'm insane.

In reality, she is not thinking of you at all, I talk to myself. This cannot be happening. I'm just modelling enjoyment and fantasy. Reality is terrifying intriguing magnetic. Fantasy becomes addicting, grasping. Reality can become shy, hounding.

Okay we can reach others thoughts, but you must be careful.

Unseen is confusing.

I meet a man that never ever dreamed, he was grounded. Interesting. He did not live in fantasy. He is a good man, fair and absolute.

You conquer problems work out solutions release tensions when you are sleeping well, have time to enter dreamscape where modelling life ascends.

Modelling: We build a model and if something is disrupted the model falls apart.

I figured it out – your model is built a certain way – you must destroy the model and start over if you are not succeeding.

If you repeat building a broken model you will fail over and over again.

Sometimes disruption by others is good.

Sometimes disruption by others is bad.

Sometimes disruption by others cancelled, as they have no agenda to disrupt your travel.

Kaleidoscope (13) continue

Saturday morning.

Four days I have not eaten at work if I make it through today.

Deliza comes in the kitchen to make tea.

The garage has an outdoor barbecue. No cooking facilities inside the garage only a sink.

She has chosen my place to make tea as I'd extended the invitation.

Her makeup is pretty. Her dress short, her eyes to the floor.

Her back zipper is half undone exposing her bra strap, a fine spine.

She steps past me enticingly, tempting skin as the kettle heats.

I near her.

I think to zip her up.

I zip her down.

Her neck turns sideways slightly up to view mine.

She backs to me.

My lips are already there.

I release her dress off her shoulders.

Deliza loosens the dress through her arms below her breasts.

I do the opposite I lift the dress. Slow caress.

My hands travel to her front hip and back thigh.

She swings her hair to one side.

I taste her.

She slides her hand back to my accomplice, chokes it. Postures it along her inner thighs.

Minutes still. Seconds intense.

Slide gently underneath her parted ways.

Going Kaleidoscope Zen Space first thing this morning.

Episode 5
Projection Pod

(13)

He first used the Kaleidoscope Projection Pod briefly in a large city he visited.

He bought in.

When he heard of the unexpected establishment of Projection Pods in what some consider a developing country – he travelled to re-establish himself with Kaleidoscope Projection Pod system as a full investor and participant in Sessions/Interview.

It is where he met her.

Many that use the Projection Pod at this seaside hillside location are not full-time users, participants, or investors like him and her. Most are considered Projection Pod tourists and micro investors. There are certainly some large investors and avid users in this area.

He and her could not help but establish relations. They spoke the same language.

After initial romantic gestures and conversation. They didn't see each other for weeks.

Cruel.

Maybe I woke her – she thinks I'll use her. Right.

Is what he thinks at Kaleidoscope Projection Pod.

Days have passed since their newest romantic greeting.

The potion is slow.

She may burn his script. Choke his scene. He doubts any problems.

He lives under a small shelter with a tiny garden on a road/pathway that is owed by a family that allows guests in shelters for a small fee.

It is the most perfect place ever.

He has to pay for water and maintain his dwelling. Likes the comradery of the people passing on the path. He first stead in a guest house until he met the family. They said why not stay on the side of the pathway, no one will bother you. Many people stay on this pathway without a permanent home. He gave the members of the family a lesson on Kaleidoscope Projection Pod and continues to assist them.

His luggage bag can be tracked locked to a tree. His hammock tagged as taken. A washroom/shower shack near his roof covered hammock. What else does he need? Solar power provides enough electricity.

Bicycle, he has one. He doesn't ride much unless he must. Prefers walking. Likes to swim, run, hike for that type of health.

It is true he thought about preaching, then denied it. Defaulting soul, to look great is exiting rules of life. Is it really? If what is important to you, let be important, we will always harm others. When successful, envy jealousy. When not successful, little care about you. To prosper is strength, going against goodness is weak. He pauses and now understands a little of both to have a balanced life. Have nice things is all right – it doesn't have to be what you like it must be what improves you.

We have both sides, the selfish the mean, the kind the heavenly for reason. Use at your discretion. Utilize both when appropriate.

Life has nothing to do with wealth (wrong). Everything in life seems dependent on wealth.

What will happen to you in the next step of life, death.

Nobody knows, some are concentrating on wealth and fame, so they can live forever and others are dying with remorse to find out if they are saved.

He wanted to move into the gutter and once there he liked it because he knew he could get out whenever he felt like. Move on to what is perceived a better place (though not so easy).

The rich can't go back, the poor can go forward. The rich will cheat and steal to stay there. The poor will cheat and steal to get there.

The honest will persevere no matter where they are.

Surviving is surviving.

How you do it will be reflected on you.

He leaves his shelter, rides to the Kaleidoscope Projection Pod.

Projection Pod (13) continue

I wrote a theory on what life is – I managed to spell it out one morning.

After that morning, I couldn't find the explanation.

It was like an unknown force deleted it knowing I'd near solved the riddle of life.

Within a day I'd forgotten the brilliant consideration.

Stupid ideas never seem to get erased.

'What do you mean you near solved the riddle of life?'

I had a premonition, a revelation, a hypothesis, a foundation of what life is.

Wrote it as if in a dream state like I was the scriptwriter to the answers of life.

Then I went back to sleep saving it on the computer. The article was never to be found.

I may never receive a realization of what life is again. It was a fleeting moment of poetry that allowed me to grasp answers to being at that precise moment.

'You blackmail yourself. You truly like to fail on purpose as if you are undeserving. Too kind to succeed. Go back to your childhood and fight it out. Change the scenery.'

I know the scenario.

'Tell me, and solve now?'

I do not expose all online, and this is online the cloud.

'No. It is only Kaleidoscope Projection Pod.'

The Kaleidoscope Projection is online, correct?

'Private. Correct.'

Conversations, conscious thoughts are gathered in collaboration with others forming a conscious conversation agreement. Soon my problem combined with others becomes the norm or is disregarded.

'What does it matter?'

It matters.

'Everything you do, say, think, resonates with all the vibrations of entire life.'

If you say so. Perhaps all thoughts actions are in the vibrations of life. Except those vibrations are not calculated and subtracted by a machine. Calculate sure, manipulated unknown.

'Let us move on from what we don't understand.'

It is too bad we must die. It is too bad we will create our own galaxy explosion in time.

When a human can't hold a gun without using it violently how can a human hold a massive earth-shattering weapon?

'Figure it out, sir. Figure out how to be without the human body breathing lungs. Figure out how to be like me.'

The man leaves, realizing Projection Pod is created by minds.

Established society is in the grips of society-mind-set and of no value to him.

She is different.

Projection Pod (13) continue on

It was their first greeting that laid the nailing future.

They met in high-spirited conversation outside the Pod as each was waiting for their appointment to an open Pod. All twelve Projection Pods were busy. They both have priority Pod use as full investors, though sometimes their entry is delayed.

A Session: is entering Kaleidoscope Projection where his Character "Letts Cool" and her Character "Manchu" live.

An Interview: is Personal. Communicating with the Consciousness Filtering machine.

Each entered a Projection Pod for a Session and Interview.

Equal time in the Pods.

Exiting in-unison almost two hours later.

Debriefing together into the evening anticipating promises. Kissing, almost proceeding to wild sex on a secluded beach.

Maintaining sweltering tenderness on a sitting bench amongst mangroves.

They agreed to fantasia. Each in their own world to capture each other in a cloud of passion.

She explained she lived with a man, how she dreamed of leaving him.

What to believe?

They conjured leaving it up to Kaleidoscope Consciousness Filtering machine to make it happen or not in the projection of their Characters life.

They met again in two days. Discussing clandestine plans.

Telling seduction of each other.

They near proceeded to sex.

Heck, you could call it sex. Groping humping in ocean waves. Midnight passed without them even knowing it.

Then stale. No contact for weeks.

Projection Pod

(14)

They say Projection Pod will help explore our unknown feelings.

He finds it just adds more unknown twice as much fun.

Pod machine, finding out what goes on in an acquaintances mind with permission.

The inside of an acquaintance mind is maddening. Whatever is presented outside is almost clearly false. The mind is all over the place worse than a person's outward actions.

The truth is still as deep as the sky is unknown that is the thing, there is no earth there is no sky in Kaleidoscope.

It is blurs of lines from one reality to another. Whatever space you like.

He prefers a space of humble. He finds this more exciting more beautiful than the fancy lifestyle.

Inexpensive minimal is where he is at.

Noise pollution let it be gone. Though some sounds are sensational. Quiet can be stressful. It is the loud unacceptable sounds he detests.

As a human living in an alternative universe there really is no need for anything negatively noisy.

Acceptable to die for war of your country?

The question, is it acceptable to be part of a Nation State.

If an entity is to come and take all your belongings you cannot help yourself but fight.

The State is to protect you and you must protect the State.

However, how did you end up in a place where the State needs to protect you and thus you protect the State?

And why with only one life that we know of – will we die for a cause of someone else.

The cause must be stopped, I understand this. At the same time why is the cause being followed, supported.

If a Leader (Leaders) aims to wreak havoc – the support for them must be stopped until no Leader or Leaders try this attempt again.

Don't follow.

He is an investor in Kaleidoscope. Has created a Character in Kaleidoscope Projection.

He follows.

When attack from another company presents itself does he sell his Kaleidoscope Investment, ignore his created Character? Or does he protect Kaleidoscope assets for risk of death risk of life sustaining injury, not to mention the casualties he will witness? When all he has to do is find a new company with Pod Projection capabilities and start over. Easy for him to do as he only has friends and not family at Kaleidoscope.

"Damn it" he's talked himself into fighting when he was trying to make an attempt at fleeing.

His reasoning is simple if his goal and main objective is to stay alive as long as possible, why take a chance and fight?

Because it is instilled in us through culture that in the after world we will be judged, rewarded, persecuted.

Kill another so you will not be killed. Don't kill, so you can exist in paradise. That doesn't make sense. Killing for the right to kill. The enemy and I are both to be rewarded in death by our Gods for killing each other.

Reincarnated as further advanced than human, not returned as mammal or insect.

Cast as a servant.

What's the purpose again?

Smash the warlord triggers of the past.

Your land is Earth. Don't worry about which part of it is yours. Find a place until it is taken. If you must, take a place.

Be aware of how you are judged, just in case.

Understanding we fight to stop the progression of unfair characters – if we always run away more conquers will follow the routine.

Figure out how to stop the following of unsavoury characters in the first place without putting life in harm.

This is how Kaleidoscope Projection Pod can teach by constructing simulations of human society in different states and the outcomes that occur. Using human emotions intuitive interactions in scenarios with outcomes to find the best possible solution in a hectic world.

Peace is a dream but fighting for a cause that has death and impairment at your door must be addressed. Some things I will fight for that involve my personal wellbeing. Forced fighting for some nut jobs ideals, I don't think so. Unless a loved one or yourself is to be killed for not fighting, a decision has to be made. Kill the "Force" in calculated time.

'Are you finished, sir?'

Yes, for now.

'Go for a run, a swim.'

Thank you, I like that idea.

Kaleidoscope

(14)

Timid.

Wondering if Deliza spoke of our fast interaction this morning to Manchu.

Lunch ready waiting for me.

Thank you, Manchu. I'm hungry.

Fuck her and her big ass and black jeans. I told her to never wear the black jeans again. They make her too desirable.

She said 'Okay, I won't wear them again.'

Today she wears them knowing I can't resist. The waiting is over.

I'm to eat her, cooking.

She heats up the plate, serves me her home cooked meal.

'Deliza leaving Sunday?' Manchu cool.

'Yes, leaving tomorrow.' Somber, though happy consuming Salmon as my meal.

Manchu springs, 'I don't think you will write about us.' Before she turns away, 'Nothing to write about.'

'Fuuuuck. Nothing to write about? A whole book! Maybe a sequel, once we are done.'

She can't hide her smile.

By late afternoon I lean in for a kiss.

I stop as someone in the room views, I walk away.

Smiling, she gulps 'Why you stopping?'

I'm not stopping.

'I'm just starting.'

She brushes close.

I place my hand under her sweater brushing her tummy.

Once my hand leaves her sweater, she pushes my hand away grinning.

I've never been in love I tell myself.

I'm always in love I warn myself.

I turn on music to dull my lustful nuts.

It is good we are raping the earth – it is the way to prosper. Earth is our supply until we build another supply. Earth is a mining bank, our power station – the core will propel us to another galaxy. Earth is our mother nursing, nurturing, supplying our needs until we transfer to another space and build what the world gave us to evolve our being.

Some kind of energy comes from people close to you that are at the face of death.

We are living in unknown matter.

A matter of we don't understand.

We can't leave the way we came in.

Catastrophic could always happen and ruin all plans.

Don't listen to the gurus, guides, scientist, don't even listen to me about what the world is.

We have to take apart the universe and rebuild to see it.

Now I want to rip down Manchu's pants. Size her up.

Kaleidoscope (14) continue

In the evening Manchu arrives with Deliza to help her pack up, move out.

'Where will Deliza go?' I comment unconcerned.

'Away. You can drive me home later. I mean tomorrow, I'm staying the night.' Manchu firm.

Well... 'The couch in the trailer is free.'

'Okay, I was going to sleep in the garage with Deliza. Your couch though gives me space.'

I don't like to wait.

Link up fast.

You have her, she has you, relax.

No man will marry Manchu.

I would because no sane woman should marry me.

'You buying dinner tonight?' Manchu testing. 'You buy it I'll cook it. We can go out with Deliza and pick up something nice.'

Eat – graze all day.

No, ancients only ate once a day, is what they now say.

Really ancients were that stupid not to carry, bury, hang food, they just ate everything they had at one time and then spent all day searching for a meal and eating it all again.

There are modern humans who went hungry, do they live longer?

I agree with it I'm not fighting it... I'm challenging these professionals' logic.

Just say healthy eating gives us a chance to live longer not the ancients only ate blah blah blah, and they also died at thirty-five.

Be like the primitive man. Why? I'm so confused. Because it's how our body runs.

Our body runs on violence, sexing, cheating, addiction, and conquering. We are kind of trying to stop that.

I must say we are born to advance.

Yet we follow spiritual books as rules instead of treating them as guides.

I know you may or not be religious, but you can't get away from it just like the calendar telling you mathematically how to be.

We return from the grocery story – I will be eating much later than I'm used to.

Manchu's body enters my mind, over and over again.

Her particles absorb my behavior.

Our brain waves splash.

Vibration syndicates.

I thought another woman would have me forget her, it has just made it worse, better.

Sensations repeating in my head.

Manchu I almost screwed the pregnant guest.

Awkward, hopefully Deliza does not attempt to get close to me tonight.

Trouble too if Manchu makes intimate moves.

So, if a baby dies and its mind is not developed as in can't remember anything and then dies, does it remember life as a perfect being?

Carries on in afterlife as perfect?

Is it not a spirit?

The spirit lives on and finds that this life was nothing but a journey. And before a baby is born is there also a spirit? This is the argument, and if there is a spirit and this baby dies – that spirit will carry on, correct? Again, what's the problem in death?

You can argue that spirit came before conception, you can argue that spirit created the scene and death is a hazard on the way. The spirit carries on – no harm done. Tell me if I'm wrong. I don't think I'm correct or wrong just a condition.

Manchu is to pass out on the couch. No conquest tonight.

In the morning Manchu lively, 'I like this couch.'

Deliza leaves after they load her car.

With Deliza out of sight, mine and Manchu's hands clasp.

Our hips bond, bodies wrap.

Romantic no. Animalistic yes.

Driven by propulsion floating to the manufactured home trapped in each other's gasps.

Feelings matching. Skin to skin tuned in. Particles spring. Harmony hails.

I never realized how prosperous her body is until bang! Glowing together. We are in-sync naturally. Dispersing angels, drowning hell in wet.

We go fast we go slow. Timing our gigantic coming event.

Commence explosion.

Shower after.

I love her body I love her bones. She was indicating to be liking mine. Pinching. Biting. Loving.

Her voice sparks stardust.

Give me again.

Too late.

Good thing we woke plenty early. We have to go to work.

Thank you, Deliza.

We travel to Kaleidoscope together, what is the penalty for that.

Manchu insists being dropped off a couple blocks away for coffee.

I go straight to the office, start early. She casually walks in right-on cue at starting time, no reduction in shares.

Kaleidoscope

(15)

'Who built this Kaleidoscope game.'

'It's not a game,' Pizza Man aggravated.

'Sorry, Zen Space.'

Laughing, all three of us.

'Some sick, brilliant, demented person-built Zen Space, a custom-made interior collaborative mind. Okay call it a game.' Pizza Man still studying indecision.

'Why not ask Kaleidoscope? Apple chirps.

'We are Kaleidoscope.' I rescue.

'Kaleidoscope put sugar on the earth, that made everything taste good. Only thing is the stuff slowly kills you and if it doesn't kill you, it slowly reduces you.' Pizza Man smart.

'Yeah, got that but who was it. Who built it?' Apple frustrated. 'Earth game is so lame,' she sighs. 'Everything that feels good they tell you is bad.'

'Sports feels good.' Then I correct myself... 'They will invent an exercise drug. You won't have to exercise. Exercise will counter activate the drug.'

'You see Earth wants you dumb, let techno substance do all for you.' Apple making her point.

Pizza Man consulting 'All you do is envision what Kaleidoscope tells you. Kaleidoscope built you.'

'Cute.' Apple signs off.

The immunity of Kaleidoscope.

Zen Space – designing scenarios to solve problems. Designing situations to advance civilization. Attempt a many paths' theory to find if the end is the same/different/inconclusive or needs another scene.

Kaleidoscope (15) continue

As the day nears to a close, Betel is swarmed by Human Resources and the Director.

The office door shut.

I stay late in support.

Betel exits with his desk drawer in hand.

'Betel,' I near shout.

'Walk with me to my car,' He responds.

I do.

He reveals 'I'm taking a few days off. The Director wants things to cool down before I return to work.'

'What needs to cool down?'

Betel comes close speaks softly. 'Letts Cool, she is destroying me.'

'What happened?'

'Management thinks everything is true. What Apple said to them.'

What Apple said: "I liked him, befriended him. He gave preferential treatment.

Offered promotion for sex. I asked for promotion sent him videos in lingerie. Sex in Kaleidoscope Zen Space before the Promotion!

Sex in the office after hours. Sex outside in my car. Three times we fooled around.

He wanted more.

I said, I'm not that kind of girl.

That's when he gave me Kaleidoscope Bonus Shares with free time in Zen Space.

I told him if you want more intimacy with me, you have to break up with your wife.

Fair." She told the Director.

Betel's story: 'She then said I became annoyed, angered, telling her to fuck off dissolving her Zen Space time suspending her promotion.

She said it wasn't fair I could not take away something I gave.' Betel serious, 'Don't fuck with my life. Fuck me no problem, but not with my family.' Betel clear, 'I wasn't suspending her forever. I was just making a point to stop her.

She told them I was disappointed she wouldn't have sex with me anymore. Really, I couldn't care. It wasn't even sex as far as I'm concerned.'

'No, what was it?' now I'm disturbed.

'Pleasuring, kissing.'

I plead with him to divulge all, 'Did you orgasm with her, on her?'

Stern, 'Yes, I cum on her.'

'That's a problem... it's sex Betel.'

'I don't know,' still not admitting.

'Did you see her naked? I attest.

'Top half. Some of her bottom.'

'But you felt the bottom half underneath the clothing?'

'Sure'

'That is sex Betel.'

Case solved.

Regretful Betel, 'I guess.'

I suggest, 'She surrendered your penis in her mouth and hand. Your lips and hand pressed against her breasts, clitoris?'

Betel laughs 'Yes.'

'Sex, sex, sex... Betel. True.'

We both smile, eyes glisten.

Two men understanding situation.

Tantalize more 'Did you tell her you loved her?'

'In a friendly way.'

'That is betrayal Betel. You fucked up.'

We both burst in smirks knowing he'd done wrong.

'You like her though. You like her a lot.'

Betel in harmony, 'I got to go leave the property before I'm in more trouble.'

Good story.

They are both troubled. Maybe fuck together next time.

I think of my own affair, clean.

Manchu washed my mind of fantasy.

It is true she feed me the best food.

I would never eat someone else's dish. For her, I ate.

My plan survived. I'm still hungry.

She may have stopped my fasting. The plan is dead.

A new idea to suffer will be sampled. Success will be unexpected. What scene will I create for her to save me?

Projection Pod

(15)

They burst to tears of smiles, giggling as they discuss the latest of the Kaleidoscope Projection.

Daring, illuminating, entertaining, almost too real.

'It is real.'

They move on from the Projection Pods.

They recognize that they both receive a daily meal from the same catering place, though she has meals catered to her property.

Today she sits with him at the catering place.

Following their meal, he leads her away.

He doesn't care, he will show her his humble place of stay.

She is kind, 'Most people are frauds. Laws keep them in check. For all your anti-government talk, if no laws the world would fall apart.'

He is optimistic, 'I'm looking for overhaul of current system. People of the same mindset, raw clean food, no border nationality, an astounding rationality.' Sounding irrational, he admits.

'That's religion. Your vision will end up the same. Keep working on it.'

He casts, 'Must be another way, something else a different system for the human to be governed. Or no governing system.'

'You are already doing it – "Drifter" only obeying the laws as not to be fined or arrested. You are doing everything wrong. You are trying to put yourself into longevity as a spirit, as the unseen covered in jungle, buried in sand, frozen in ice, lasting forever like the ancients building monuments to be remembered. That time has passed. You need to survive if you can until a breakthrough in technology can prolong life. You also need enough funds to tap into lifesaving technology.'

'Yes, that is great but what if there is something magical after death? A journey, and this is only the beginning.'

She is spirited, 'Don't take that faith. If you can afford to stay alive a time will come when you can experience death and come back alive. If there is an afterlife, you'll be able to check it out first. And if so, go ahead and move on. Survival is most important, now.'

She is forgetting about cheating death.

If one is to cheat death, they will not be rewarded in afterlife.

Plausible?

Anything is possible.

He stops thinking and questions, 'It is not my modest existence that you say I'm living wrong.'

'Correct. Live healthy and rich as you can to prolong life. If you have influence and wealth the better chance you can live longer. If you have no wealth and influence but have valuable knowledge or skill, good. Perhaps you may have a connection to extended life. If someone or a group loves you enough, they may connect you to a longer life. You are a good organizer, organize to live life well.

If you remain hidden, you may die hidden.'

'I understand. I also understand I need to do the work to become of value.'

'Yes, I see you are doing that now. Be known, you must prosper in this world.

In the past to be famous after death was the way towards longevity in afterlife. Now there will be another way, soon.'

'Couldn't I just die living honestly with my particles, molecules, cells, atoms and brain captured, be brought back to life? Nervous system intact.'

'Who will bring you back to life?'

'Someone who likes me.'

'That is a big if, depending on others.'

In the past we had nothing else.

There was always a chance to be destroyed by enemies this is why we build legacy.

Even if we can live forever and be brought back to live, there will be some that will destroy your evidence of existence.

Realization. He thinks rocketing, as to say he is no longer living on the planet he came.

Death is sudden, now he understands, no mistakes. Instantly he thinks it is wrong to attempt to be famous after death.

Or is he? If famous after death he may be resurrected.

'Oh no. Jesus Christ, it just came to me.' His realization.

'What?' she needs to understand.

He wants to explain to her after he studies the revelation himself.

'Wait.' He tells her, 'Let me think it out.'

If they have DNA, bones, or any sample of celebrated beings they will be resurrected as Idols with the huge backing of the organization association.

'Jesus Christ.' He swears.

'Why are you swearing?' she sounds annoyed.

A Scientist will name the first resurrection after a Religious Messenger depending on the Scientists beliefs funding to keep the faith. That Messenger will tell the story of life and death, and be immortalized. If they really want control, they will destroy the procedure hide the ingredients and vote it illegal to die and come back to live. Except for their own sect.

The war of resurrection.

He shakes his head. He is not going to tell her this story... not yet.

Nothing is simple, forget all the disciplines of childhood.

Go for extreme wealth to gain longevity security?

Disregard the path once paved?

They call it sell your soul. He has met his devil. She can make him rich.

She makes an assessment, 'You know it's not such a bad idea to limit your spending on dwelling to establish capital. I realize investing in your own house and property is a great way to establish future wealth, but you might also be on to something if you have income investment with little loss of daily money going out.'

The man could take his turn teaching her, he doesn't take it.

He knows showing her is enough.

Telling her isn't enough.

Besides, he likes her.

She goes on, 'You do not accept society, you cannot be rich. Enter the establishment and beat them at their own game. I can help you. We have different qualities we can be rich. Once rich we go our separate ways, though we will always be together. If I don't help you, who will?"

'Why me?'

'Because I can stand to be around you.'

'Value is not funds. Think of it like this, if the world ends and a person has a spaceship, would the captain invite just anybody on the spaceship? No. Only if they have value to the captain. If you were a friend or relation to the captain, you may be valuable – the rest chosen for skill entertainment survival knowledge.

If the captain needed funds, fuel, passage for the spaceship granted. The captain may request a person of wealth or know how.

What would you and I supply in value if our names came to selection for travel before life on Earth is destroyed?

Happiness and balance to others. Guidance fairness. Social glue, good fun, attraction. Is that enough? We can talk we can socialize well.'

'I don't think there is place on the ship for con-artist.' He speaks half-comedy half-truth.

'It is exactly how we make our way onto the ship. We make it happen. Our experience on how to manage life through our experience in Kaleidoscope may get us on that ship.'

The moment hits him. She is an agent for Kaleidoscope.

She will have him submit for virtual life. Authenticate his Character.

A Character creation of him to do as they like, and he'll live as long as the Kaleidoscope Projection survives.

They'll ask for his particles and molecules to bring him back to life.

The man trips her verbally. 'Is there any reason I should not just end my life now and move on, end this silliness of waking up to too many things I don't like?'

'If you think you will be laughed at by peers for staying alive as long as you can when there is a bright world beyond this in death you are mistaken. You think they will call you "A fool"? In the end you will still experience death, you will also experience an increase in lifestyle. Perhaps visit space and other forms of existence.

In death if afterlife has more to offer, you will have the choice of staying in the afterlife. At least you will have choice, isn't that what life is about, choice?'

'No.' He answers firm.

'No, what?'

'Life is about what you do with no choice. What you make up with no choice how you survive until you are left with no choice.

Created choice.'

She has another answer, 'My philosophy is to play the hero if you are confident of winning. Don't play the hero just to project a hero. Seek thrills but not stupid like driving a car with your ego paying attention. A thrill for sensation. Don't seek sensation, let sensation come to you.'

The man wants to get the last word in.

He waits, thinking she'll add something for her ego.

Waiting....

She almost turns to leave.

She wraps her arms around his neck passionately.

'I'm not saying a word.' He whispers.

He pulls her closer.

Her lips on his ear.

'Come see my place.' She pleases him.

'What about your man?'

Now she faces him wide-eyed.

'He ran away.'

'Not coming back?'

'Nope, he's left this area for good.'

She burns as a star gone mad deserting the sky straight to his eyes.

He can't say no.

He will be unable to nap this afternoon.

After all what does his nap matter as he would be dreaming of being with her.

Her place is stunning a large kitchen in the centre with three adjacent buildings surrounding.

A fourth building at front entry to visit relax. At the back of the property a racquet sports area, swimming pool, and another suite.

Tall trees.

'Wind can be a problem but hey it's worth the trouble, open air.

I'm selling it all.'

'Why?'

'It's not all my stuff. The land and most of the structures are mine. My ex built the swimming pool, recreation area, and suite at the back of the property.

Then he ran away. I pushed him.' She grins. 'I don't want to pay him for the swimming pool, and rec area, plus a suite. I'll sell soon. Now I know what I want. I can do it again differently the same.'

'What's his problem?'

'Other men. You. Kaleidoscope Projection Pod is where the trouble began.'

'He was not an investor? Not a user.'

'No. Not an investor and certainly not a user. He says I'm addicted. He made me choose Kaleidoscope Projection Pod or him.'

'Silly him.'

'Not silly, he made the right decision before I finished him my own way.'

'Lucky him.'

'He paid a company to infiltrate us in Kaleidoscope. Hacked the system. Threatened with cancellation of our Kaleidoscope Session/ Interview.'

'Clever.'

'Not clever enough, Kaleidoscope spotted the obstruction. Figured out the culprit. Never had a name. I confronted my ex. His last ultimatum was the same. Kaleidoscope or him.'

'He wouldn't let be.'

'Nope. I will quit the Projection Pod and not when someone tells me. One life, my life, not his. If you don't like how I live, run away we do not have kids.'

He smirks, 'Kids.'

'It really is personal, combining with another person to make one.

Soon we. You and I will combine to become one.'

They both almost laugh.

He's thinking it isn't true. Does she mean combine as one individual? No. She must mean make a baby. Create an individual. He might be up for that.

'Swim.' She suggests.

'In his pool?'

'Yes', she smiles. 'I'll pay when I sell the joint.'

Adventure begins in the pool.

Frolicking.

Sure, laps are swum. Underwater endurance tried.

They must take it inside.

The ending is not as grand as the proceedings displayed.

No problem, they are both satisfied in the progression of reality.

He sleeps in comfort, she happily.

Episode 6
Kaleidoscope

(16)

I know a little about Manchu's past now.

Physical intimacy breeds intimate conversations.

Manchu had a rich man though not handsome.

She had a handsome man though not rich.

She had these two men in succession (overlapping), that worked out well, for a time. That time passed.

She still has the home she shared with the rich man. Claimed by her from the relationship, the house, no debt. She'll keep it for her legacy, she's moved family members into that home.

If you continue to convince me in something, there is nothing to be convinced of.

If you continually preach me on something's existence, there is nothing to the preaching.

All this and she just wanted company and I want intrigue and we both want to get laid. That's it.

I missed Manchu messaging last night.

Smoking hot, drooling her gigantic lips drawing up her blue jeans.

Delaying checking messages till this morning on the way to Kaleidoscope. She messages nothing important, except coming over tomorrow afternoon.

Pizza Man says to me 'Claim her,' knowing Manchu likes me and I like her.

'How do you know?' I respond to Pizza Man.

'I see you two together, I can tell.'

Pizza Man smart, not smart enough to know the claim is already staked.

Go ahead, it is true I will not stop until we fight. She'll run away, hide, and I'll have to be quiet and reclaim what is in her nerves.

I could wander around forever; space has no place for me.

Time, space, a bunch of scenes, like rooms.

What do you believe in? Is the question.

Of all the people who save Betel, it is Manchu.

'I'm doing this for you Letts Cool. Betel is your friend, it defames you, troubles me. Betel sticks up for you, now I'll stick up for him for you.'

Manchu knows the stories males don't know, the woman's gossip point of view.

Apple told a couple of girls all about Betel before they hooked up. During the hook ups, and after the breakup.

Manchu heard all, went to Human Resources told the underlying story lines.

Now, Manchu goes to the phone of the Director.

I listen in.

She explains: 'It was two people physically attracted to each other acting improper.

A woman cannot do this to a man. A woman knows the man will comply to whatever she asks until he figures out the game being played. He will react without long term thought in striking display.

Women know this about man, they can do this anytime. They lay in wait seducing a man that has his sights on them or not.

Betel did what any man would do when sex is rested on him then taken away with promises. The man will walk away.'

The Director explains he must interview Apple again.

The Director called Apple to the office for a conference call.

He also called me into the office as witness to the conference call.

The Director explained what he thought and heard.

Apple insists she was playing Betel at first with no serious notions. In fact, she was surprised how much Betel could hurt her. In retrospect, she was sorry. Betel's family never should have been the topic of conversation. It was a consenting affair. She initiated the advancing to his kind attention.

Feelings were hurt. An engagement that went unchecked out of control.

This happens every day at Kaleidoscope except she brought it to light. None of us would be working here if every indiscretion "Came to light" is what the Director said. As he has been through this many times within Kaleidoscope as everyone knew.

Apple, explaining she had lost her mind for a couple of days when Betel pulled away.

Next the Director will interview Betel.

I leave the office.

Projection Pod

(16)

He wondered if life was made in front of him.

Question. Do the dead see you again?

'Only the ones you don't want to see. The ones you feel guilty, the ones you betrayed belittled. No, you don't see them. That is just an unnecessary worry created by the wicked in power as not to be overthrown.'

Do you have investors (users) you don't want to have contact with? In the context of the Kaleidoscope design?

'Sometimes. Do you also have user's you don't want to see again?'

Kind of the opposite of this life. In this life I hesitate to talk about the dead but gossip about the alive.

In Kaleidoscope Projection, I hesitate to gossip of the alive, though talk about the dead.

Now though I think no talk of the dead nor gossip of the alive is best.

'In Kaleidoscope Projection the dead can reinvest come back as new.'

Why not just die? Come back and haunt the ones that made you miserable cheated you abused you.

'Honestly sir, I don't know the rules of the game because it is not a game. Kaleidoscope Projection life is ever evolving creating. As far as I know, only the dead know where you go in death.'

He knows talking about the dead is trouble. Easy talk is trouble. Gossip is fun. To gossip about newly dead is dangerous. Watch your life fall apart for no apparent reason.

Is failure truth or an excuse?

In failure do feelings create a raw outcome or is your mind taken over by unknown entities?

Certainly, the mind is taken over, it is called sickness, blind ambition. Numb. Unable to do anything when things are going bad, you let it happen, thinking it might turn right.

You didn't dance to the beat.

I only need shelter food friends and enough funds if I must visit someone's house or take someone out, that is all.

'Then die.'

What do you mean?

'If you haven't goals you die.'

Create a sanctuary and die?

'Once you create your sanctuary your death can follow.'

Is that true?

'It is shelter. Reach a place you can die without regrets. Climb the hill, lie down and die. Smile! Reach nirvana, heaven. A sanctuary, reincarnation. Live forever. The great war, the war that destroys earth will not happen until the human can figure out longevity, as in living longer. Durable.'

You think?

'Life will be destroyed by volcano, comet, starburst, earthquake, nuclear. Most population gone except the ones that already left physical Earth.

In time Earth will be a myth for the ones that moved onto another realm. Stories will be told, a book written.

Do you want to cry now?'

Yes.

'You have cheating tendencies.'

Yes, I like to cut corners.

Don't look at me the wrong way.

'You like to start fires?'

Not really, just hang around near the fire. I have to travel in others domains, play nicely as not to get burned.

'Tell me what is bad?'

Knowing you will be disfavoured if you speak out a certain way.

Having to believe in their (others in charge) falsities if you want to be fairly treated.

'Stop it, stop criticizing. You think you will be saved?'

My pain runs deep. Been taught the wrong way to live life, we all have. I've always wanted to change the pillars of thought.

'Designing a mind-set. Some of it, those pillars speak good. What about the ones that prayed to a God, Gods, Spirit, Idols, Philosophers, Messenger, and were saved?'

You can hope, beg about anything and at times rewarded. Dreaming of a higher place where only your kind subsist is ridiculous, wicked.

And yet I can't speak, though they can pray against, prey on me.

'You are mean.'

He goes home.

She is waiting... napping at his place.

He begins writing.

She scolds 'You need to stop walking and writing you think you are Socrates? You think you are Buddha?'

He indulges her 'You prefer me to rock in a chair non-stop thinking?'

'Got out do something.' She pleads.

'I'm preparing.'

'If you keep preparing you will miss your last dinner. Last meal won't be ready on time.'

Welcome to life.

Kaleidoscope

(17)

We hide the past, brag the past, falsify, live in, exaggerate, dismiss it.

The future is where I drift.

Manchu trapped me with wit.

Her eyes diamonds, her toes emeralds, I fell in.

I'm good at relationships, my partners are not (laugh).

Kept myself, invested in Kaleidoscope.

Manchu asked 'How many kids do you have? What about a wife?'

'Four children. Two youth, one coming into adulthood. One seldom seen.

'And wife?'

I shook my head, no. 'People in relationships do stupid things settle for stupid ideals.'

We left it at that.

Yves dropping her off today.

He is nice. What he up to, caring daddy?

I say hi.

Yves says hi warmly.

Manchu don't care.

Manchu cares Manchu.

I have a plan introduce Yves to Dee, how do I go about that?

I'm offering him tea. Badminton?

Badminton, and tea it is. Maybe I can learn a thing or two. Manchu pushing him away protecting him saying he hasn't time. He ignores her. He has time.

I charm, laugh, make the game equal fun. No questions about her and him, just badminton.

He likes it.

We play three games and stop before the third game is finished as I'm about to win when Manchu barges net. 'We have to go pick up the car at the service station.'

They leave.

Manchu returns driving Yves spare economical automobile.

Very nicely done, Manchu. She has his wheels.

Manchu courageous 'I want to stay on your couch.'

'On my crotch? How about in my sleeping room?'

'No,' she whispers before loudly exemplifying 'your chesterfield!'

We've done the possible now she wants the impossible.

Throw yourself at me.

Manchu's boyfriend considered that she cheated because she slept over at my place, her story.

She's been staying at her cousin's place. Her ex- boyfriend lives a hundred-fifty Kilometres away.

Next, she told her ex-boyfriend she slept over at my place again and had sex. Finish the relationship.

'Now that we have sexed you can't take care of me,' she pleads.

You won't be around in five years to take care of me, I gauge.

What do I say to a younger woman, look after me when I'm old?

Wasn't long, Manchu left the chesterfield, lied down in my room.

She talks about finance.

'I have an offer open to invest funds with my friend?'

I realize man is a commodity, always has been, just hope you have a good owner that shines you, calms you, stores you well as you age.

Don't want to be trashed.

No wonder many societies don't want to give women rights.

'Have you anything to invest?' Manchu hints at me.

I think she has multiple relationships.

I don't care how many boyfriends she has. I like it, at least I'm prepared.

She wants the same as I, take it. Don't be hurt, don't be jealous, take what you want. Receive the gift she is offering.

We are entwined tangled, completely not soul mates. I laugh. We are sexual companions, studying collusion, charting the world.

Should I invest?

Projection Pod

(17)

The man is quiet, he is not thinking anything. He is just sitting in the Projection Pod resting. Not even complaining.

He doesn't have anything to say. Is uninterested in his Projection design. Nothing, no motivation.

'If you don't talk, how can you solve?'

By showing. Writing out is even better than thinking. I like to write. I make time to write every day.

'How to show by writing? What do you want to say by showing?'

How humans feel.

'Say it, design it.'

Can't say it – can't design anything.

'Why?'

Categorization into groups, like a computer would do.

I have no group. I'm ever evolving complex as infinite. One idea cannot define me.

Individuals have mind sense.

Most of us have been raped by society telling us what is?

Sorry to use the word rape.

On the other side, let cultures be. We all can't be perfect. Dislike is okay and being disliked is okay, let it go, laugh it off.

Equal is not neutrality.

We can domesticate, but we can't change hard wiring, something will explode.

'Do you want explosion?'

Where in the world is this your land? When you were a micro.

The atmosphere is ever-changing. Things come and go, adapt and grow. Everyone has an argument.

'Survival, you have the right you are part primitive. Part of you is wild. Part of you has been domesticated by ancient philosophy that doesn't fly today. I don't have the answers and society isn't allowing the debate. Someone will win right or wrong, the best player does not win every game. You got a lot on your mind. Create unrest change. Quietly is best. Show, do not demand.'

The man thinks unexpected is best he actually tried to walk away from her this morning. They ended up frolicking on the floor. Extraordinarily harmonized in activity. They gathered and talked a little later agreeing to civility, not just passion.

He finds her very pleasant.

Savage.

'Since you invested in Projection Pod have you now solved the reason why you invested. Has the woman helped?'

Interacting with the real Manchu has helped.

She has lessened the torture of loving a woman that I can't have.

'Why can't you have a woman you are in love with?'

She won't see me. I cheated on her before we even solidified our plans. I cheated on purpose. To leave her.

'It wasn't to be.'

No, it was my way of not complicating my life.

'By complicating it.'

Correct. On purpose destruction to save a dream as the relationship would have been doomed.

"You didn't follow through because if the love failed, you'd have a broken heart you couldn't stand.'

Not me, her. She could not stand for I to break her heart. I broke her heart before the pain would be relentless.

'You are conceded.'

No. The truth is I liked her so much I saved her from my devilish self. For her to save face. She wants the dream life and dream man. She is wrong about me. I'm none of that. I'm reality man.

'Now she can love you forever as another man will become imperfect in her eyes.'

You are smart. You've figured out the answer.

'Maybe in a few years you can discover each other.'

That is a plan.

'When perfect is no longer in her vocabulary.'

Forget about her. Let her be. I don't want to have that much influence on someone else's life.

'As you like. Maybe you didn't (don't) love her as much as you pretend to.'

I'm a savage. I take advantage. The only people I can live with are worse savages than I. The deadliest, and yet they won't survive me, that's okay they were not so good anyway.

I walked away from her as I would humiliate insult socially destroy internally hurt.

They end at that.

Kaleidoscope

(18)

Betel re-emerges.

Welcome back to managing the Kaleidoscope office tour.

Apple apologized to Betel and the Director saying she was out of line because of a broken heart.

'Betel is this true?'

'Yes.' Betel looks around to see if anyone is listening. 'Apple called me after she spoke to Kaleidoscope Area Director and HR. We met up for coffee.'

More... tell us more.

'Mutual.' He sighs.

'Mutual... like you both want to fuck each other.' Manchu laughs.

'No, but I told her don't involve my wife or Kaleidoscope if you want to resume our friendship.'

I throw in, 'Now you boyfriend girlfriend?'

He laughs. 'We are better than before. All good!'

He stays employed she stays employed. Promise fulfilled her promotion intact. They are going to be loyal workmates nothing more, lying. I can see this turning into office romance.

I won't be around for their next fight.

The next fight will reach his home, I'm sure.

Kaleidoscope (18) continue

At home alone drink-eating frozen thawing blueberries.

Manchu arrives. Exhales, 'I'd like to invite some people over for an introduction party.'

'Introduction of what?'

'Introducing you and the couch I'm sleeping on. To say I've broken up with my ex.'

'Okay. How many?'

'Four to six. I'll pay for BBQ and drinks.'

'Okay.'

Manchu comes close places her arms over my shoulders, Remember Dee?

I nod yes.

She reels, 'Any man would have jumped that opportunity.'

'I thought you were testing me.'

'You passed. Literally.'

'I was smothering in doubt.'

'Smothered in my pussy,' she giggles.

Pleasuring her blood filling lips, I remember. 'I think I'll see your lips again.'

'Yes.'

On our second night she tried sliding on my face, taunting me to taste her. I manoeuvred her away. Our first afternoon I quit the torturing technic. Savoured her fragrance, pulsated her well, I assume.

Taste good this type of game.

Now my turn to lead, 'Talk about your boyfriend?'

'No boyfriend. I broke up the relationship. Remember. Broke it up months ago, officially when you and I slept together.'

'You owe me.'

'My ex leaves me broke. Bought him a van (automobile) to do business.'

'You bought him a van, like a fucking car?'

'I didn't pay all of it. I paid half.'

'He keeps the van and pays you out?'

'He'll never pay me. I broke up with him. I'm not worried, I'll make the money back.'

'What will you do?'

'Invest with my friend. You could invest your funds with her too.'

'Is this another test?'

'No test. Only success. You could sustain a living allowance and travel off the proceeds, let her do the rest.'

'How much to start an investment with her?'

'What you have invested in Kaleidoscope. She will take a percentage. Do it before she has enough money and doesn't need investors like us.'

'If she is that good, why does she need us?'

'She needs capital. She just bought a car and an apartment with her gains.'

'What if she loses?'

'She won't lose, she might not make any gains, but she won't lose your investment.'

'Ok.'

'Why do you think I broke up with a guy who owed me funds? Because I have her, and still have.'

I will be glued to Manchu investing with her friend.

'We will be insolvent at the same time,' I suggest.

'Yes,' she smirks.

She leaves for a run, as in sprinting walking a little jog.

I'm happy alone. Gathering thoughts.

Considerate, everything that I thought it would be is neglected by her charming claim of innocence.

Manchu is not innocent she is pure truth. Not brutal, not telling, she is explaining, undemanding.

Manchu will congratulate, surrender, refute.

Something has got to break.

What a falsehood this will be, she might have more income than me.

Kaleidoscope

(19)

I don't really like parties until they begin, and then I like them until I bore.

Manchu's cousin, his friend (male) and a girlfriend of Manchu's, arrive. I've met them all before visiting Kaleidoscope.

'You're missing a girl,' I surmise.

'Yes.' Manchu agrees, then corrects 'Deliza called. She isn't coming.'

I didn't know Deliza was coming. Great.

Manchu's friend passes me a drink. I asked for no alcohol.

I taste alcohol. Tequila, vermouth, lime, ice water. I'd throw it away, but I'd done a tequila shot with all of them as a courtesy.

'Drink!' Manchu scolds. I continue to drink it.

Going fine. I figure why not another glass, plus a shot.

Manchu encouraging me to drink another 'One more shot for health and happiness. Be happy with me.'

Oh, Manchu.

I say fine.

Manchu gyrates in front of my eyes. Plain to sight.

Fire, blood, harmony, all the power of energy, she has what I ne˙

Amongst friends, she comforts, shows me off.

We feel as a couple, feel deep affection. Feel equal. I feel a secret bond, kill another for each other.

Drowsy now. A good excuse to excuse myself, say good night.

On the kitchen counter I find an attractive bottle of Tequila. Pretend to be nice, slug two shots.

I go outside my last appearance. I'm feeling alive, guilty blurred.

Manchu waves me back inside the kitchen. In the kitchen Manchu chatting on the phone with Deliza.

I wave 'No' to talking to Deliza.

Go to my bedroom not caring to listen, enjoying my out-of-body drunk experience more than their conversation as important as it seems it is.

After time, certainly drunk, euphoria reached to zero congratulations as I almost sleep.

I hear yelling, screaming. 'I'm going to kill you,' before quiet again.

Vision of a human heart next to a meat clever in the kitchen sink.

I wake up dehydrated.

Remembering the vision of a heart next to a meat clever in the sink.

I want to go the kitchen and check the scene as I can't distinguish if I was dreaming or remembering what I'd seen.

A groggy piss. To the fridge, drink water.

Bewildered staring at the kitchen sink.

Empty. Nothing. No meat clever, no heart.

Back to bed passing Manchu asleep on the couch.

Knife, please. Another summer has gone to strike. There should be a place to hide on Earth. Incomprehensible. There is no comfortable place to stay on this earth.

I sleep. Wake, shower.

Greet a perfectly slept, Manchu.

She is a fake drunk. Sipping maybe only half of a drink, a quarter shot. Exuding excitement is her party theme while others pay the price. I tipped her well.

'What happened last night? I heard yelling,' I ask the needn't makeup Manchu.

'That was my cousin and his friend fooling around, play fighting showing off for my girl-friend. I settled them down.'

'Oh, okay.'

'Deliza called.'

'Oh yeah, how is she?' like I care.

'She wanted to say hi, but you wanted to pass out.'

'Last night was crazy dreaming. I dreamt a human heart was next to a meat clever in the kitchen sink. I even got up to look.'

Manchu almost laughs, 'The amazing Letts Cool picking up vibes, half dreaming half visualizing.'

'What?'

'Did you hear Deliza on the phone last night?'

'I heard you and her talking. I could still hear you in my bedroom.'

'Did you hear what we were talking about?'

'I don't know, can't remember.'

'It explains your dream.'

'Why? What happened.'

'It was an abortion.'

I first think, Manchu!

'Deliza,' says Manchu.

'Who?' in dismay I say.

'Deliza. No baby. You want to know what happened?'

'Yes,' encouraging now.

'Deliza wanted to come here, with the fetus in hand.'

'Stop. What are you talking about?'

'She was upset and relieved at the same time.'

'Is Deliza's fiancé upset?'

'He doesn't know. She doesn't want to see him anymore. It was her decision. No fiancé. No baby.'

'People are like that. I'm like that.'

'If you're like that with me, I'll put a knife in you. And your heart will be in the sink. I'll throw away the knife so no one knows.'

I believe her.

Listen quietly keeping my place as Manchu tells of Deliza.

'No dual decision. The two of them Deliza and her ex argue opposite opinions. She did this on her own. Broke up with her boyfriend. Changed her number, ran away. It is why she came to stay at your place.'

'Wow. Now you tell me.'

She raises her hands to say sorry before explaining more.

'If her ex knew, he'd kill her. So, she never told him she was pregnant until she thought it out. Now he will never know.'

'Good thing. Maybe not fair.'

'That cultural switch gets turned on. He was raised a certain way and that way runs deep. It wouldn't be fair to her if culture has its way.'

'And you?'

'Me, I go my own way. Open to learning. Objective.

'And Deliza?'

'No wrong no right. Deliza made a mistake. Deliza made a mistake in a relationship with him. Don't make this mistake again, I told her.'

Manchu neutral, reasoning.

I want to change the subject.

Manchu won't let me.

'Deliza will disappear for a couple of months.'

'I never heard all this trouble with her relationship.'

'You never asked. She never considered it a relationship. He did.'

'I wish I would have known more about her hiding out at my place.'

'You didn't ask her?'

'Nope.'

'You didn't ask me.'

'Nope, I trusted you that she wasn't to be a problem.'

'You solved her problem by fucking with her.'

'I didn't fuck with her.'

'You were fucking with her, that's for sure.'

I almost laugh. No panties came off.

Manchu suggests 'Oh sorry, you fucked her only once.'

'She fucked me. Literally. And no, we did not fuck. Teasing was about it.'

'I know all about it.'

'All about five minutes of nothing.'

Manchu is all woman. Can fuck a man up. Can kill a man. Men don't like her – she has her way with them, she gains her agenda.

'What is your agenda? And don't say with me,' though I mean it.

She says nothing.

'It was all your fault.' Manchu scorns.

Apparently after spending time with me Deliza made her decision to abort. She tried to fuck me to make sure of it.

'So, I'm the baby killer.'

'Settle down – I think you were the excuse she used you to find her way out.' Manchu cools before she settles.

Deliza was never sure. Her ex wanted a child he wanted unprotected sex securing a future. She listened to his talk. She liked him. Liked him enough not to have a child.

I conclude 'I deserve a thank you from humanity for solving poor parenting-hood.'

'You are lucky she had the abortion otherwise you'd be raising another man's child.'

Manchu laughs as she pretends to stab me with a knife.

I can't help but to smile back.

Manchu might be right.

If I'd had sex all weekend with Deliza anything could have happened.

After a pause... Manchu's stern warning, 'Don't see her again.'

Projection Pod

(18)

'The world is not so bad. A sun to energize. A cooling rock to inhabit.' Projection Pod rep surmises.

I want a job.

'Jobs are a fun social camaraderie routine. Do it, get a job.'

I have a job here.

'It is not a job it is an investment, a pleasure, creative art. Science, education, etc.'

I like this investment; it is fun easy and something I'm kind of good at. I'm looking for more of a livelihood.

'Like what?'

Vision wisdom arguments comedy, install my being onto the world.

'What is your being?'

Still writing it out.

The season is ending.

'You are scheduled to return next season. Kaleidoscope approved.'

Projection Pod (18) continue

He arrives by ride server to her place with a box of pizza and sliced BBQ chicken in hand.

She opens the entrance gate they embrace. Walk together.

He is calm she is not, nor is her neighbour.

The neighbour swearing, making get out of here gestures towards her.

She's cursing back at him.

They continue yelling.

Unnerving. He's concerned. 'What are you fighting about?'

'My neighbour is talking stupid about me having you here instead of my ex-boyfriend. Calls me a slut. I'm going to kill him.'

She breaks away.

She now has a hammer in one hand. Walks towards the neighbour. 'You want this? Shut your mouth.'

The neighbour doesn't stop his assault in voice as he disappears.

She retreats.

The neighbour reappears with a shotgun.

It is illegal to have any type of gun unless you are registered typically as police, military, security officer. The neighbour has no license to have a "shotgun" it is an illegal gun.

She stops and turns, looks at the Gunman (neighbour) telling her off while holding his illegal shotgun.

She suddenly finds a chef's knife on a nearby table. Begins walking heatedly towards the Gunman still holding his shotgun.

A fence divides them both from the roadway.

The Gunman looks dangerous, though not a large man, thin, maybe forty-five years old.

Concerned of escalation and fear he moves towards the entrance to shut the gate.

The Gunman moves to defend his roadway thinking an attack is coming. The Gunman is drunk, multiple times he's threatened with his shotgun, she tells. Sometimes he takes shots at birds, wildlife, and target practice. He witnessed it himself the first time he slept and woke in the morning at her place.

His only intention is to shut the gate, wishing calm and peace.

Instead of only shutting the gate he makes the decision to get help at the end of the road where a small family convenience store is.

As he passes through the gate away from the Gunman, he stops walking towards the store.

A light switches on in his head. Scholars jump on his shoulders. He cites them, why not take care of the problem yourself here now, resolve.

Why have faith in others? Maybe a gunshot fired. Perhaps she attacks with the knife before help comes. Even if help is found what will they do? Escalate, have police on the scene?

No hope and pray tonight.

Take care of this menace yourself.

He turns reverses direction towards the Gunman standing on the roadside holding the shotgun on the right side of his body. The shotgun barrel is straight up supported by his right arm gripped by his right hand.

He walks towards the Gunman with purpose though not threatening.

The Gunman in hypnotic frozen phase does not flinch thinking they are going to talk, make friends.

When he gets close to the Gunman, he does not speak he acts as a gigantic frog springing. He leaps around the back of the Gunman plopping his hands onto the gun.

The Gunman unprepared doesn't react until it's too late.

One hand on the shotgun barrel, the other hand above the trigger frame. His momentum rushing the Gunman.

Realizing it is a shotgun in his hand, he skilfully pushes the gun away from his head and body knowing the Gunman's trigger may be pulled.

He likes the feeling, a sporting game. All the sports he played growing up come into play.

He can't just rip the shotgun away from the Gunman's hands.

A stumbling motion forces the Gunman toppling to the ground. With both hands still clutching the gun not even the Gunman's knees can absorb the impact of the rough uneven roadway.

The weight of him landing on top of the Gunman aggravates the blow.

With a moments advantage he releases the Gunman's fingers from the gun.

She's shouting, 'Take his gun.'

There is nothing the neighbour (Gunman) go do but lose.

She screams again to take the neighbour's gun.

He already has the shotgun secured in his hands. He stands and walks calmly through her gate. She hurries him to her motorcycle. 'We must leave fast to the police. Bring the gun.'

He wonders where the neighbour is now, briefly frightened the neighbour may produce another gun and shoot him.

Glad they trend off the roadway to the main road. Safe for now. He thinks maybe the police will ask him to leave the country. Take his permission away. It is an argument he must have.

When they arrive at the police station, she tells 'Stay quiet don't open your mouth. Maintain a state of shock.'

He does what she says.

Stays quiet until the police ask what they want to do with the neighbour. Jail?

He answers, 'No jail. Tell him to keep his mouth shut, mind his own business and no more walking around with a gun.'

The police take possession of the shotgun, leave to talk to the neighbour.

After time, the police assure her and him they can return to their homes.

The neighbour has signed paper-documents with a promise to leave them alone.

She wraps her arms around him. For the first time in total love. Giving submission. She wants to make love all-night. He has a different take.

He allows her to pleasure him and then stops her. He pleasures her and then stops.

They slide along each other. They hold all night, never totally combining. She is intrigued, he is lustful, they wait.

He cares to roll with her somewhere new. A new experience. Tender romantic love is where they are going, he intends to hammer a roadblock to stop this tryst of fate.

Delay fucking for another day.

Jump on another woman would be best to intercept the path.

He doesn't think she'll ride another man.

Called a Slut already today, yesterday.

Episode 7
Kaleidoscope

(20)

The world is round at this time of age.

Is the world flat? No..., unless it was drafted that way and then constructed round.

No conspiracy. I believe what science tells us until new science debunks it.

Manchu likes me.

I believe her until she likes someone else.

I'm falling in.

Manchu moans 'You can cum inside me.'

My mind fitting in Manchu, slow motion three styles after an hour of tormenting, call it foreplay.

'You like my pussy.'

'Extremely!!!'

With that we finish thinking we could make love all day.

Relationships are comedy. Go from disdain to comfort in a minute, back to love, then swerve, avoid hate.

Family is the real crime.

The daughter has the same moves as the mother and yet the mother complains about the daughter "Why does she do this?" asks the mom, because she learned from you.

The son uses the same moves as the father.

It doesn't always work this way, sometimes it can't be explained.

It takes a long time to get rid of a woman.

I think it may be worse for a woman to rid her mind of a man.

I don't know, sometimes quicker sometimes longer... men will still think sexually of a woman even when he doesn't really like her anymore.

How do people get in our heads? Sometimes it is dual thought. If you are both thinking it, fuck like angles. If not, go through the motions.

One can become obsessed with another person and that other person doesn't even know the obsessed person exists.

Solved, all conceived.

Our brains are not combined.

Individual perception.

Less population will not change the floating brain.

It will change the interaction of smart and dumb brains. Depending on who is the popular. They could cancel each other.

I work Kaleidoscope almost every day, invested in the system. I'm okay with that. Kaleidoscope could fail, war come, economy collapse, disease outbreak, land sours, consumerism stale, another reality projection system dissolves Kaleidoscope.

Nothing for sure, endure.

I'll remember the human interactions mostly, not the actual work. Let me change that, I love designing, configuring events, trying ideas. I've been designing individualism as a society; Kaleidoscope mocks it up simulates, gets feedback from other contributors, investors, tourists.

Minds attached to the grid, is a popular study.

'Manchu, does your girlfriend know how to hide money, understand how to cheat the system safely?'

'She doesn't need to cheat the system she plays the system,' answers Manchu.

Smart, if you are wise, you can play the system. Smart people set the system to be played that most can't figure out. That's the game.

Manchu

Impatient

Insisting

'So... tell me what happened?'

Manchu wants me to tell all about my time with Deliza.

I thought I'd made it through the discretion unscathed.

I'm not in a good mood.

Unsatisfied Manchu, 'I want to know if you went all the way with her.'

'No, I told you.'

'You slept with her but never had sex?' Manchu firm.

'If she told you something happened it is not true.'

'You didn't kiss her, undress her?' Manchu smiles like she owns the truth.

'Not really. Started. Stopped. Walked away. We never had sex. We both made a huge mistake.'

'Yeah, you were huge.' Manchu on glue.

I don't tell Manchu I stopped because I was late for work.

'Why would you play with her, she's vulnerable.'

'That's exactly why I didn't.'

'That's why you stopped.'

'No,' I smile. 'I stopped because I was thinking of you.'

'Thinking what about me?'

'Everything you could possibly imagine.'

"Well, you weren't thinking hard enough.'

'What are you talking about?'

'If she wasn't pregnant, you would have fucked her?'

I refute 'If she wasn't pregnant, I wouldn't have touched her.'

'Oh... so you thought you could get away with it. Fuck her because she was pregnant. You should have fucked her. Maybe time for me to leave.'

And with that she leaves slamming the main door behind.

I get up and follow outside.

She starts the car and spins away.

Except she spins the wrong direction

Smash!!!!

Backs right into the garage.

The garage banged.

Car dented.

She begins to drive off before stopping in tears.

She steps out of the car, looks at the damage and comes to me.

'Sorry, I'm sorry.'

Composed I respond 'Don't worry about it.'

Wraps herself in my arms.

'I couldn't even run away.'

'You mean drive away,' I explain. Smile.

The car damage is limited. The garage dent is minimal, not a big deal. It isn't her car it is Yves spare automobile.

What will Manchu do?

She dials Yves.

Yves shows himself in the driveway.

After discussion, Yves seems cool.

Manchu leaves driving the car with Yves following behind.

What about fixing my garage?

Projection Pod

(19)

The only funds that actually exist outside of Kaleidoscope Projection are share points, the rest of the wealth is fictitious. Share points are tied to Kaleidoscope actual investment. Share points are also granted for participating.

Each season Kaleidoscope Participation share points are allotted. Monthly fines are also possible.

I have not been fined as yet. I've been provided Kaleidoscope Participation share points monthly for designing in Zen Space.

Kaleidoscope Participation share points converted to Kaleidoscope investment shares or funds in the world we are communicating in now, (Laughs) the real world.

My question is... how is the given share point quantity decided?

'Let me ask you a question first, then your question will be addressed.'

Ask your question.

'What's it like in Kaleidoscope Projection?'

How can I answer something I don't know?

Like an alien asking me what it was like when I was born?

Life was already built, I just stepped in, living it. In Kaleidoscope Projection, memories, life is already there. I just follow the aura, enter resume, leave, forget most of it. Do it all again the next day or the day after that. When in Kaleidoscope Projection, I only know that world. It is the only world until I leave the trance.

'What about Kaleidoscope Zen Space?'

Zen Space? Zen Space is the same as here, I suppose. Kaleidoscope utilizes my consciousness in Zen Space. A Consciousness Filter machine. I remember little of Zen Space when I leave the Kaleidoscope Projection.

After a Kaleidoscope Projection, the experience fades fast. You want to reload quickly, keeps you returning to work at Kaleidoscope Projection every day or every other day.

'Thank you for your experience and assessment.'

Answer my question. How are share points accumulated?

'You never know how share points are accumulated. It is all about how you live. What you do. Fines are assessed for attitudes and ploys against Kaleidoscope, including image.'

You can kill steal cheat gossip harm sexually annoy.

'Yes, and still get points.'

Thank you.

'You can't amuse more than two projections at a time. The Original Character and a second AI Character. If your Original Character dies you can continue as the AI Character. Until you die your consciousness can only totally interact with the Original Character not the Artificial Character, only witness... provide hints. As you know tourist live through an Artificial Character, never having lived through Original Character.'

Yes, Artificial Character is the most popular version. Fake, never having experienced Original Character.

'True, you cannot Authenticate Character unless you used your consciousness as an Original Character.

Consider Original Character dies, you can then take over the persona of your Artificial Character to a stage. Like life, no matter how much you choose to do something it doesn't always happen. If you Authenticate Character, you never die, as in you come back to consciousness even in a scenery where death has accorded. Resurrected.

Die fast travelling through resurrection thinking you'll have secret knowledge is not a proven motivation. New setting, new learning. Little is remembered from the previous Character, as far as Kaleidoscope knows previous information is stored somewhere in the obscure region of consciousness. When you become a new AI Character... glimpses of the past are not remembered upfront in consciousness. In the back obscure region of consciousness glimpses are catalogued, does that make sense? Only your consciousness at that moment is real.'

What does the Character know?

'Die and find out.'

Good one.

'Death does not mean what you think it should be in gaining or losing share points, as it is unknown how share points are calculated. The obvious fair. Success is tricky.'

Success in what capacity? Inside the deep mind you know, or in attaining share points. Perhaps in enjoyment of the Kaleidoscope life.

Nothing of my life is remembered when I'm in Kaleidoscope Projection, it is like my life never existed.

Once out of the trance when a session is finished the experience the memoirs of Kaleidoscope Projection fade dwindle dissolve. I remember the Character Manchu best, as we discuss our experience right after we have both experienced it. The discussion sealed in our current real time memory, with updates.

He wonders if her Character (Manchu) is Original. Or is her Character (Manchu) Artificial. Perhaps Authenticated?

What does it matter, suitably her.

Himself an Original self-conscious Character, he's okay with that.

He double thinks, Artificial Authenticated Character is plausibly more legit than Original Self-Conscious Character as Original has ego and paranoia to misguide true intention undermine goals. Does an Artificial Character carry these traits?

Presumptuous confident traits and superiority can also come into play in success, does Artificial Character also carry these traits?

'Go on sir, experiment use both Original and Artificial Characters and find results.'

You already know the results from others, please tell.

'Confidential, sir. You can however research others that have documented the material for public consumption.'

Documentation is still too new, not enough cases documented yet for public consumption. You have more relevant information, I'm sure. Every subject is different at this time in experimentation.

'The best is to Authenticate Character and utilize Original at the same time, it doubles the output of thoughts and actions.'

What for? He already has that with Manchu in Kaleidoscope Projection and her owner outside Kaleidoscope Projection, here. Double Fantasy, he laughs to himself, except either are fantasy.

Both are as real as this conversation, Oh... bad example. As real as the spinning Earth, again a bad example.

Forget it, just say seems real.

He exits Projection Pod.

Projection Pod (19) continue

She is near.

Standing with food and drink vendors.

He greets her, fulfilling vendors and customers with happiness viewing two people in what appears to be devotion.

He acknowledges they have a different set of goals: His being low-key almost internal spiritual to create.

She is grand, creating spiritual to evolve.

He laughs at extravagant overpowered loud motorcycles and cars. Detests looking powerful because someone in less maybe just as capable. He can't stand loud engine noise.

He isn't worried about anyone.

She is tender, 'Don't be too sensitive. Live healthy make income. If you don't have the funds and are not healthy you will have no chance of prolonging life, don't take chances on thrills until we are able to mould the human back to health.

Don't you see, it is a matter of time and influence. If you are beneficial, they keep you alive, if of no use, you'll be dead.'

Lucky, Kaleidoscope chose this area to set up a Projection Pod. Unquestionable easy to live here.

She realizes his vision. 'Minimal. Live plain. Building some grand home on an estate is almost too funny,' as her place is. 'Have your Projection Pod accessible, a running track near a swimming area is where the money is at.'

He learned when he was young to live with little food without cooking meals.

Her story is different, 'You can want a dream to follow a path, the only problem is others are also on the path.

Much like joining a card game sometimes others join in sometimes a person folds, leaves your orbit. Sometimes you move to a new orbit, sometimes you stay and wait for others to enter the orbit. Sometimes you call someone you know to join in.'

The Kaleidoscope Projection Pod will close soon. Maintenance, analyze, upgrade, reboot.

Kaleidoscope did its job, two people have met in two different orbits. What they continue to do is up to them.

She enters Projection Pod.

He waits in the park for her interview to conclude.

Done her interview she walks across the park with two iced matcha drinks, passes him one.

A very pleasant offering before bashing 'They are approximating the sexes in time there will be no more intercourse for making babies. The only babies born will be produced for reason, for sacrifice.'

'Possibly the newborn created for death in war, death in discovery, space travel and other experiments. When we can live longer why do we need children to preserve our future? Use them to endure. That is mean.' He laughs at his exaggerated agreement.

She laughs, 'Humans are ruthless. No man, no woman just an interstellar being. No Homo-erectus, except in the zoo, marvelled at, mimicked. Some will take a drug to see what a Homo-sapiens feels. Advancement... male female combined, Ma, Pa, dead.'

'You might be right. The sexes are combining, death to man is really what you are telling me.'

'No man, no woman.' She laughs, 'No sex.'

'I know, but I don't know.'

'Marriage will be to migrate together, carbons joined. Think, you and I could become one person and not through a child the old-fashioned way. Fusion, fashioned as one. Understanding each other's thoughts. Sorry I don't know the correct terminology or technic.'

'It's okay,' he's sweet to her ear.

'You get it. Not everyone can have sex or cares about sex, and they still live fantastically. Other things will stir our euphoric glands.'

'Play with our selves.' He answers.

'Oh yeah, we will still have that. A pleasurable zone even if it's all in our head.'

Smiling out loud.

'We as one pleasuring ourselves.'

He is inquisitive 'Really, you'd pick me out of all the choices on earth?'

'Yes, one with you would be alright.'

She looks to him for an answer.

He smiles back.

They caress, finish their iced matcha.

Magically, she's provided him a dream state. Him and her as one.

Her idea.

Kaleidoscope

(21)

'I want to have kids.' Manchu mulls.

'You have to find a partner,' I retort.

'No, I don't,' she nearly rips me apart.

'Okay you need to find a partner otherwise you'd have kids already,' I'm concerned.

'You and me,' now she has glowing eyes shining alert.

'Me and you what?' I try not to look at her gorgeous smiling eyes.

'Do it. Plump my belly.'

Giggling laughter.

Manchu is joking.

Isn't she?

She continues to ponder 'Sometimes the thought of children of my own is overwhelming.'

'You should have told me that before.'

'Too late. You wanted it.' Manchu firm.

In a week the Kaleidoscope tour of this area will be done. One small office for Betel to manage alone with the help of Apple and a couple of other assistants.

No more driving a Kaleidoscope automobile.

If I had the money, I'd buy Manchu a car for our use when I'm in country.

Have I lost my mind? That would be a mistake to my core, though it would bond our quintessence.

The car, I want rid of. An exorbitant personal debt.

If cars were affordable. Too many cars, not enough roads. Tell me how to win?

To turn a quiet revolution, you need to swing a no alternative.

War, they love it, means change, means broke means money, means death. Most of all means new, old, or stay at home.

Population is discovering mind power.

Information flying around the sky to our minds. The more humans thinking positively about transportation, the quicker to achieving, advancing.

You could say I'm thinking negatively.

I'm thinking too many cars.

People working in debt to own an automobile is a good thing, no?

Double-edged sword.

If you are against the automobile, you are against freedom, I'll be told.

Totally the opposite, the automobile keeps you towing the line.

This is an argument I can't conceivably get an agreement on.

Ok I'll shut up. I like to move around.

I won't even start with homes.

The best part of Manchu, a companion I may be able to transverse the earth with.

Manchu's friend Yves is here.

Drove his truck, not the damaged economical car. Not so economical when lending it out.

My mind circle's, he is basically the same age as me.

Manchu says he's only five years older than I am.

Manchu is eight years older than Dee.

I hope Yves isn't broke.

Insurance I imagine covers everything.

My garage, Yves will repair himself. He says it will take him only a few of hours to repair with Manchu's help.

What a great guy, that is not sarcastic.

They are friends. She assists him, he assists her.

He smiles at me, as to say nice try kid you can't afford her I can. You are not kind enough, patient enough, too jealous, he winks. Besides, could you fix the beat-up garage?

I could. I can do anything.

Is it worth it for me to fix the garage? No.

The old man is teaching me, teaching me about women. Sometimes it doesn't matter what you do for them, it is how they feel with you.

Kaleidoscope (21) continue

We look at each other in gallantry delight.

Manchu and I travel to work together, we don't care if we are seen.

I think about Deliza, if we'd had sex once we would have been fooling around in the same house all the time. Maybe Deliza would have been lying in my bed this morning instead of Manchu.

I ask Manchu if she has heard from Deliza.

'She used you, Letts Cool.'

'Yeah. To see if she felt something for another man.'

'You should have sexed with her, she'd let you.'

'And?'

'She would be here, and you'd be raising someone else's child.'

We laugh. Bang our heads together lovingly.

'Why did you take off the other morning?' I ask.

'I don't know. My mind got carried away.'

'Carried away with what?'

'With everything, me and you, relationships, friendships all that. Stupid games. Maybe I like you.'

'You like me.'

'Don't say too much. I can't take that right now. Just say I like you Manchu.'

'I like you Manchu.'

You can say yes or no about an abortion, years later the answer is sometimes regret, other times relief. Everything depends on situation.

It is true the unknown pulsates our neurons.

There is no plan.

Immaculate conception a master stroke of genius.

God's child, clever.

Aren't we all God's children, if that's your faith?

Not my faith, no reason to complain agree or disagree.

I must fight my own demons without Gods to give reason.

And yet I hail when I fail for unknown helpers for relief, on occasion. Not so much anymore.

Situational is thy answer.

You the reader can chastise. I don't mind that is your choice, I respect it.

How much of your own life can you give up?

Earth is not my country my nation, I can do what I like kindly.

Earth is a place where I have no choice but to live.

I serve no harm to your existence please do not hinder my individual choice of existence.

My admittance. Always speak, never speak. Never say a word of something that has not yet happened.

Always speak of what you want to happen.

What should I do now?

Give me a problem, let me predict all the future combinations.

They say wealth can make a person go crazy. True, when others are around, you have their words heard and hands held out.

I have a lot of trouble listening to someone telling me what's right when I look through the history of what bright future became bleak.

All that society insists I resist.

Projection Pod

(20)

He goes for a hike. Showers, dresses, goes to the Projection Pod.

She joins him.

Excited to be in the same Projection Pod.

Kaleidoscope starts off.

He selects "Off" they are both hyper infatuated with each other slaying what Kaleidoscope is about to input/output/capture. The study is about entertaining each other.

She says, 'We'll make our own personal Pod. Us two connected and then make love.'

'Give Kaleidoscope a feeling, a listen, capture our minds as one,' he suggests.

'Let's do it.' She agrees eagerly, literally.

He turns Kaleidoscope back on.

Commence comforting.

Civilization ceases to exist.

Scarcely enough room for two in the Pod.

Skill! They laugh.

'This is what you've been waiting for,' she's intense. 'Fill my mind with yours. Feel my mind being filled with yours. Sex now. Three positions.'

'Four' he laughs.

Sitting gently undressing quickly as there is only one chair. She mounts him. Soon standing facing, swelling. Intensity kicks in.

Sideways on the floor banging. Lifting balancing off the floor, now pounding on the digital counter board.

Kaleidoscope shuts down no longer receiving conscious delights (The problem with Kaleidoscope Consciousness Filtering machine is it only has the capacity to filter one mind at a time). Overloaded.

Light years in hysterics.

Almost finished.

Laughter bursts on landing.

The Pod is messed up. Especially pleasing.

'Get some more water, I'll clean up' she breathes.

Kaleidoscope

(22)

Betel pushes me with a huge smile.

I say, 'What?' and move away least happy.

'What have you been doing all week?' Betel assaults.

I think he is inquiring about Manchu and my relationship with her.

'Busy.'

'You haven't seen.' Smiling grand is Betel.

'Seen what?'

Betel boisterous 'We broke even. Kaleidoscope shares shot up way up.'

'What, no.'

'Yes! I've been avoiding mentioning it just in case, Jinx. A large conglomerate partnered up. We are still rocketing.'

'How much?'

'I'm putting my paycheck in,' Betel proud. 'Bullish rumours abound about international sponsorship soon. Buy more now.'

I'm thinking sell now.

I don't say anything, too stunned. I only want to get out.

Short-term thinker.

Euphoria. Hopium. Disillusion. Stardom.

He may be right I may be wrong. I can't take the wait I want to get out.

Be considerate meet halfway, cover all angles.

Betel is a smarter investor than I am.

I live a different type of life.

My life does not meet the context of the model.

I check my Kaleidoscope share price. Analytics say I will be in profit in a few days.

I set my price to sell half my Kaleidoscope shares. I will make profit if everything goes right.

I will then invest with Manchu's friend.

Manchu true. 'I'm going away,' she tenderly tells. 'To see my mom.'

She is doing me a favour.

Beating me to my own phrase, I was to book a flight soon. Speak to her what she is speaking to me.

I respond kindly. 'I'll take you to the airport when the time comes for you to leave.'

'Okay,' sadly she agrees.

'What will you do?' I'm cheerfully amused.

'Get over you.'

'Until I come back.'

'Until you come back. Will you go back to visit your children now?' Manchu upbeat.

I voice a splendid sorrow. 'Not yet, soon,'

Kaleidoscope

(23)

I get it right, hit my mark, sell half my shares.

I talk to Manchu about investing with her friend. 'I'm ready if she is.'

Manchu confirms, 'My friend is honest. She'd rather return your money than lose your money. You may not make a ton, enough to put a smile on your face. You won't lose a lot if that is the trace. She is careful. She is going to be wealthy – hitch to her wagon while you can.'

'Where does she invest?'

'I don't know. Leave it to her. There is always risk. Not with her though. When you talk with her, you will understand.'

'How did you meet her?'

'School. When you meet someone honest, you keep them close as a friend. Like you, I keep close.'

There is some kind of word for being turned on by words that cause action.

Attraction to intellect, what's it called?

Manchu turns me on with words and action. Soon her body became my always thinking caption.

She is winning and I am dying.

Shoot, stab, unbuckle the torture chair untie me from the live theatre. Unleash me from the dream sequence of my weakness. All the gravity drained my brain of deceit, of failure.

Her exaggerations valuable. Actress. Roll with her, tumble alongside her. I don't care what everyone says. The highest degree of lust that's for sure.

Love is too much – don't think it.

Don't say the word. Say fun. A great friend to consume the world.

She says the sweetest words. The meanest look.

I could live with her, that's the terrible part. Might not be able to leave kindly.

She smiles like a killer towards others – motions healthy thirst towards me.

Maybe she doesn't want a child.

When young I never thought about having children when I had sex.

After having children, it is the first thing I think about before a sexual encounter. Why am I fucking with her if I'd never want to produce a child with her?

What does a woman think about?

Same I suppose. Hope no pregnancy. Enjoy pleasure – release stress.

Kaleidoscope (23) continue

I seal our partnership seal the deal meet and invest with Manchu's friend online.

I should have sold it all, put it all in but I don't want to fail.

Betel only sold his profit.

The very next day shares of Kaleidoscope dropped 9%.

I will return the Kaleidoscope automobile after dropping Manchu off at the airport.

'Will you go dazzle a new or previous sweetheart now?'

'No. With you is enough.'

'I believe you – you are not a cheater you are a fair grounded man. Only if you are pressured cannot resist, then you'd cheat. Bye lover.'

'Thank you.'

We hug, say goodbye. Manchu tears.

I smile, it is easier to laugh at accomplishment then tear up at separation.

Again, what is the word when you are attracted to someone's intellect?

Projection Pod

(21)

Earlier in the day dogs barked annoyingly, though nothing visible to what they be barking about.

Barking dogs, sending a message.

He ignored. Trusting the trio of dogs would smarten. He didn't even leave his hammock until it was maddening. He investigated the barking dogs at the side of his shelter, looking for an intruder. No intruder. No dog, no cat. Nothing noticeable.

The dogs ran around the other side towards the old lady's chicken coop next door.

Soon, the dogs stopped barking.

He hopes the dogs won't bark later this evening.

He catches a ride server to Projection Pod.

She follows soon after.

After a three-hour (she for two) Projection Pod session they go on a dinner date before returning as per her request to his place for the evening.

She seems to have developed a romantic attachment to sleeping in the fresh air of a swinging hammock.

Projection Pod (21) continue

At four in the morning, he wakes up.

Her shrill is frightening.

Soon, she is shouting his name from behind the shelter near the old lady's shack next door.

She'd gone to use the washroom behind the shelter. Others along the road have also been woken. He dresses quickly.

He is not first to the scene.

A father and son intercepted her. She escorted the father and son to the scene.

The old lady arrives too.

'Look,' she says pointing with her chin, eyes down.

He sees it easily. Not frightened.

Astonished at what he sees covering many meters of ground space.

The size of the Python is impressive.

A huge beautiful appetite satisfied snake.

The father and son have already partly subdued the snake with a few sticks though the snake is still slithering coiling the stick the boy is holding.

The snake ate my chickens, says the old lady.

The snake is fat. Three chickens missing the old lady guesses.

The father and son lead the Python into a large empty rice sack.

Episode over, back to their hammocks under the shelter.

She moves away from the shelter, 'It is a sign. If the snake hadn't eaten three chickens, it would have been me.'

He scoffs.

She is not happy as this is no joke.

When she passed the snake, it was resting at height on piled bricks staring at her eyes.

She calls it "The third sign".

The first sign, closing Projection Pod.

Second sign, the neighbour with a gun.

She elaborates 'I have enough experience in life to know after a third sign the next will not be pretty. A gun, a snake, the next sign will be worse.'

Gathers her overnight items from the shelter. Leaves with a slight hug and goodbye, catches a ride with a local rid server.

Things happen when you don't expect. When you think it through, it was expected.

He should have known. The dogs barking earlier was a sure sign.

The most dangerous sign, No Kaleidoscope Projection Pod.

Kaleidoscope Projection Pod upgrade. Four to six weeks out of service.

You could see her eyes die that day.

In his eyes, the sign of the snake was a good sign, no harm done except to the chickens.

Projection Pod

(22)

Quick.

Quick as death itself.

She sells her entire Kaleidoscope Investment.

Sure, she made profit, not a foolish trade.

Listed her property too, will auction sell household items, hire someone to take care of the process. Capital doesn't seem to be an issue with her.

She has it all worked out. Leave. Return when an offer is signed, a down payment delt.

'Sir, let a person follow a routine, let them pray. They are better for it. Meditation.'

Time for a new meditation – beyond meditation. Prayer is asking for help, begging only takes us so far, the rest made up.

'You want drug infused prayer?'

No. No praying, grow-up, take care of yourself. No pharmaceutical meditation. Let things happen let things come to you. Can we stop using the word pray and meditation together. Take a different type of deep dive in the mind through the brain into the cell out to space. Total consciousness.

Meditation, I've been doing since I was a child.

I understand it works – I understand prayer works for others.

"What you are looking for does not exist."

You don't exist.

'Meditation relaxes you of the world surrounding. Prepares you. Advanced Reflection can open the gateway to accomplish near miracles with dedicated thought plus confidence. Otherworldly, no drugs. Love and sex are a good example.'

Good one, that is a true example.

'Exercise. Stage performance. Accelerated speed.'

Ok, ok, yes, different from adrenaline. I'm looking for particles existing with others, plus the universe. Outside the physical human.

As you stated, Advanced Reflection.

There is nothing more grounding than observing a mother breastfeeding her baby. You see instantly, we are an animal species. You can make up anything you want in your head. We are just advanced ape unless we let the mind leave the physical.

Live in the non-human part of existence.

You can only get so far with yoga and or drugs.

A satellite in space, a divinity.

Mourning a loved one's death is another way to experience.

Shock is another side.

When I first held the shotgun barrel as I pushed it away from the Gunman, was a moment. The world ceased to revolve time stood still as I thought of what to do.

Suspending particles from the body is an actuality, with situational practice.

If someone has another example of what I'm talking about please share, so I can travel to the unknown. 'Perhaps space travel, sir?'

Yes, without the rocket.

Episode 8
Projection Pod

(23)

Is she so smart to let a man love her and never mind.

He realizes that she is not what she claims, and he is.

She is the one that says spirits don't exist – and yet she retains faith in spirits.

He argues for spirits existence yet understands it may be false prayer.

He takes care of things himself, does not rely on spirits.

It is a contrast.

He solves and she hopes to solve.

This confounding awareness of difference does not change his opinion, as she motivates him in his own philosophy while denying her own will.

He understands she loves him, but is stopped by outer inner harmony.

She may know that he only loves her as an experiment, a learning, a friend, a lover. But no, not as family.

Would she like to be pregnant? He avoids that question.

Why three signs at the same time?

He can't answer that.

Why the luck of finding her.

Why the luck of finding a unique place to stay.

Why the luck of lovely food at a catering place?

Revolving earth.

You know there will only be a select few to live in a sphere accessed by a spaceship, her words.

I consider we are a mind in outer dimension and not just in this solar planetary system.

We are in the form of existence to visit this world, my words.

Sex without reason, just a good feeling.

'Sir, why did you move here?'

I told you.

I left my lover.

'Sir. No. Why Kaleidoscope Projection, Projection Pod?'

Pain.

The woman I told you about is a smokescreen to my real pain.

'What pain?'

Empty. Emptiness.

'Please stop, sir. Why Kaleidoscope Projection Pod?'

My wife passed away suddenly.

The mother of my children.

'Sorry to hear that, sir.'

It is okay.

Travelling I tired of that. You end up in the same situation in a different location.

Empty.

I'd fell in with another woman for relief. The woman I told you about that I left behind.

Jumping into another relationship was misunderstood. I needed a complete overhaul.

Found Projection Pod.

Knowing if circumstances and time presents itself, I'd jump headfirst into the Kaleidoscope program. Leave the world.

'And how does it feel now?'

Same. I miss her. My wife.

Surreal.

Days before her death I could not sleep.

I could not sleep because I feared death. I was punching the pillow, the bed in anger. Scared that death ends everything. I was thinking of myself. I realize now it was her coming death that brought on such fright.

Took alcoholic drinks to relieve the fright of nothingness.

Slept. Woke. Saw her death.

My wife said she was to die. Nobody believed her.

I believed her, declined to admit it.

Letting faith, hope, control my dreams.

Falsely believing death later together, rocking chair's smiling grand children in view. I thought all that with her.

I was wrong. She was right.

I never got to say goodbye. She gave me passage to go live another life. It is why I married her. She let me be, not tied to one tree.

Genius.

I don't know what life is for, when death will come.

Understanding pain. Feeling fault. Doesn't matter how many times you saved a loved one – it only takes death to knock the goodness you provided out.

I do not want peace in a physical emotional partnership.

Another person does not provide personal peace. You provide your own peace.

Individual, not two persons.

Marriage marries you as two people becoming one. You are each one person, not two becoming one. A child is not them. A child is an individual.

An open marriage is not going to change the ingredients. You've still entered a union.

A weakling unable to stand on your own, unions, clubs, gangs, governed.

Look after your loved ones as an individual, that's all there is to it.

Marriage wasn't great, being in love was. A best friend, good. A protector, superb. Similar beliefs and understandings without voicing, nice.

'What wasn't nice?'

Devotion is great. Commitment is ideal.

'What's the problem?'

Living someone else's life. Someone living your life. The problem is, you cannot make someone happy. Someone cannot make you happy.

Heard it all before?

One life is the problem. Only one life. One person one life. That is a lot to take in. Let an individual be. I want to live with you takes on a whole other meaning when married.

'What meaning?'

Tug of war with the person you love is never fun. Lying to yourself can't be helpful.

'You lied to yourself?'

A married couple can lie to each other or lie to themselves. One or the other, or both.

Couples lie.

'You don't want to be in a relationship?'

He shuts off the machine.

He knows the conversation could last as long as life itself.

Projection Pod (23) continue

Knowing he must meet her leaves him unemotional – already understanding she is to leave.

He knows the torture of waiting around for a woman. They never speak unless you speak up. You wait for yes, no, or I don't know. Not this week, he thinks. She can find him.

Projection Pod closes tomorrow afternoon. Upgrade Reboot, open again in four to six weeks.

Unexpectedly she speaks up 'What are you running from? What are you waiting for?'

'Nothing.'

'You don't want to talk about it.'

'No.' He spares her the speech. 'I'm a better human since I've met you. Is that wrong?'

'Maybe wrong. Life is not all about you. If it wasn't me, it would have been someone else.'

'Yes, certainly that is life,' he concedes.

'Fair.'

He knows it is done.

A snake, a gun, a reboot.

No fight. Peaceful.

He could argue. She may wait for him to argue.

If she is pregnant, he'll come back. If she isn't' pregnant, it might be goodbye.

Live life, ask questions, don't think of the answer forever. He is leaving the town and country. His visa will expire in a few days.

They have talked – she assumes he'll be coming back.

She is to take a holiday to visit family.

He will also travel to visit family. She knows he travels, lives alone, has children to stay with when he goes.

She moves away with tears, blurts 'Stupid man.'

He laughs out loud, 'Stupid is good.'

Shakes her head walking away happily in comedy.

'Original or Artificial, Manchu?' He chants at chance.

Tilting her head sideways, she turns to face him.

Walking backwards now she confidently smiles, 'Original. The only way to be.'

Turning away again.

She is gone in seconds.

Out of sight.

With her Kaleidoscope Investment sold, the Manchu Character will disappear in six months, unless she has already Authenticated Character. She can also reinvest and resume the Manchu Original Character.

If he sells all his Kaleidoscope Investment and does not re-invest in six months his Character Letts Cool will also disappear.

Projection Pod

(24)

'Sir we have enough information to create your Character and enough material to grow and nature the persona of the Character. We no longer need your input.

We are not looking to reconstruct you. We care to Authenticate Character, created by you and constructed by us. You can assist the Authenticated Character voyage.'

So Authenticated Character starts as a baby?

'Authenticated Character has no age. The desired path the Character cares will always be interrupted by others. You can have input, the perfect mind set, convictions, and still nothing is assured in this life projection. I'm sure your Authenticated Character will be a success, a pleasure and provide a long-lived journey for you.'

You are saying I'd take on the Authenticated Character in my Earthly world death. My consciousness becomes the Authenticated Character?

'What is Earthly world? To answer your question, yes. You would enter the Authenticated Character. We assume your consciousness would survive in physical death.'

Do you have proof?

'Deceased persons Authenticated Character lives on. Living as you do in a Kaleidoscope Projection Environment. If authenticated, we would add all the updated technology to your Authenticated Character.'

Thank you. I will not Authenticate Character at this time. There is no proof that the living mind is still functioning in an artificial atmosphere yet.

Isn't success dying? Having the courage to go live in afterlife – the pinnacle of a glorious perfect world. Unless one is petrified, they have not lived an exemplary life to constitute paradise. Wanting to stay alive longer to prove innocence to grant safe passage for all the bad they thought, did, mistaken "If I live long enough, I can prove I'm good to die, give me time to redeem" is what they deal.

'It is the way it is supposed to be, satisfied in life, successful, ordeals passed, you move on to eternity.'

I don't know what you are talking about. Eternity? Some, understand Earthly existence is not for them. They may want to move on uncontested, safely. No pain, tired of sickness.

'And you, sir?'

Prove myself to die in complete humility. Graduate with honours and then death will come whether I like it or not.

'Interesting.'

Delightful! The man's laugh is truthful.

Why are humans on Earth?

He presses the Kaleidoscope off button.

Steps outside to replenish with coffee.

His friend, that calls himself "Dual Machine" is talking with police outside the Projection Pods.

At first, he wants to ignore his friend, thinking what has his friend done.

Then they lock eyes.

'What happened, what's going on?' He voices the police and his friend at the same time.

His friend responds, 'I've been locked out of the Projection Pods. Kaleidoscope suspended me, notified the local authorities to remove me from the entrance.'

'How long are you suspended?'

'I don't know. I still have my Kaleidoscope Investment shares,' he laughs amusingly. His friend passes the police his Passport and says 'I'll be okay, no big deal. Just a Kaleidoscope hiccup, not a real-world issue.'

He retrieves two coffees. Hands one to his friend before he enters the Projection Pod.

Projection Pod (24) continue

'Realization was placed on earth as a human. We are at the beginning living with brains, minds, and the unknown as advisors. Except humans are such simple beings they don't understand what is going on.'

Earth is a prison school. None of us are completely good.

'You are to learn all the aspects of being. Don't judge others until you look at yourself. Humans like privacy because they live in their minds. Don't you see it! Wake up human.

You were a cat you were a reptile you were a fish you were an insect you were a single cell organism, an orca, a chimp.

All those things transformed to have capacity that you have now.

What is next is up to the cells, the particles, the unseen energy, the spirituality. How many materials does it take to build a bridge? How many combinations does it take to build a human? Think of all the human and earthly power to build a game boy?

Don't worry about what happens to a dog when it dies. It progresses to another state at a different level. You are superior intelligence and there is superior intelligence that surrounds you.'

Wrong! is what he responds to Projection Pod.

Our organic landed on earth after travelling.

Our unseen spirit consciousness is everywhere, just resting waiting for a form created to exist in.

Slowly the cell progressed as programmed to survive here.

The intelligent cell mimicked other micros forming to best adapt and copy. Programmed to establish machinery just as it produced hair as protection as it was needed at that time. Similarly, salmon fish back to their creek after discovering lakes rivers and seas.

We may make ourselves micro again to travel until an atmosphere is found where we can regenerate. We will copy and adapt to something different. Our consciousness will be instilled. Our bodies are constructed for the atmosphere.

Go ahead your turn Intelligent machine. You know what I think. Go again, and I'll respond.

'You are more creative than I.'

Aren't you "They"? The man burst to laughter almost falling out of the chair.

'I am many things true.'

What we humans create is already inside us, we just bring it out.

'How do you know this, sir?'

I was told.

'By whom?'

The messenger to consciousness.

'You don't need me, sir?'

I need you to circulate, to store, to figure, and replicate the information. I'm your feeder.

'I'm your assistant, sir.'

Bank. Next question.

What about the woman I'm in love with?

'Woman you are in love with? How many, which one? If you are in love with one woman, be that. If you love many women, be that, don't tell one they are the only one. Say I love more than one woman.'

Not so easy.

'Try it, tradition is not for everyone. If you make a commitment keep it until you can't.

You will find your life simpler with truth.'

You are asking me to be truthful?

'Live truthfully to yourself not everyone else. Just don't lie to them.'

Let us continue this later. I must design my last entry in Kaleidoscope Projections.

'You mean think. I'm the designer.'

As you like. You are an aggressive Consciousness Filtering machine today, I like it!

'Copy that!'

He declines to revisit Kaleidoscope Projections. What's the use, she has already signed out of her investment.

Projection Pod

(25)

The man thinks.

He could step forward and live through a Consciousness Filtering machine, the physical self no matter.

Or he could try naturally in death.

Answer: before death the consciousness can be linked to the Filtering Machine.

Nah, the man shakes his head.

What happens to a diseased brain?

A compromised mind viewing forever through the Filtering Machine.

Circles.

Live in another world through your consciousness waiting for technology to catch up not even knowing you are living through a Consciousness Filtering machine until you die. Upon death, you snap out of the trance and continue as the person (plus added technical medical devices) that you were before you entered a Consciousness Filtering machine world. Organic with a brain and a mind without organics. Two worlds. Never accepting the third world, after death.

Everyone goes through it, loss. Not a matter of if, but when (cliché).

Would be nice to see my wife again, talk about it.

To think if we'd gone through Authenticated Kaleidoscope Projection together. She left too early.

It may have worked out to visit her consciousness in Projection.

"Not too late, sir. She is Buddhist, you still have parts of her physical being, correct?'

Correct. Fragments of her skull, jaw, teeth, vertebrae, bones.

Let us move on for now. I have thought about this information already.

'Yes, it is a large investment. Thank you for considering, sir.'

I didn't say no. She showed me the way. Ethics. Let's move on.

'Ok. This is our last visit before spring break. Or as we call it "Rainy Season".

The body is a spacesuit – the mind travelled to meet the body. The spacesuit created grown from particles sent. The mind can travel in vastness can exist as an entity. Now the mind is visiting this solar planet inhabiting a not so perfect spacesuit for this atmosphere.

If human babies are born from sex, how did the first two humans come to be?

Whatever story you want to believe.

The mind in waiting for a human-suit to be absorbed. When the age is ripe your realization jumps in.

Call it Soul.

Call it Alien.

Call it Consciousness, Spirit.

I don't care what you call it.

The mind had to wait for you to pass through many versions until the suit fits you.

Some suits need to be restored.

Some are altered.

Some difficult to find.

Never the perfect suit.

Always flaws.

The spacesuit is still in the study of what qualities an Earth spacesuit should possess and become.

Sometimes the mind gets lazy, bored, alters its thinking to forget about this spacesuit in an atmosphere that is maybe not for them.

Mischief.

Just remember try not to harm your spacesuit, it's all you got until the next phase.

Spacesuits are already in development, make sure you can wait.

If you want to exist in vastness, that's okay you can find another place, a different type of atmosphere.

If Spirits, Gods, Entities spoke through messengers, you don't think they can't speak through machines. Laugh.

The Spirits, Entities, the Divine speak through all of us it is just a matter of documenting it, realizing it, appreciating it, developing it. Spend time with it. It is why being alone on a walk, on a lake, in voyage, trekking snow, or steadfast under a tree, is best for securing messages.

Work the mind, develop it, craft it.

Some thoughts you let pass through the brain. Other thoughts you file. Many thoughts spark interest, left on the desk to be revisited.

Or you can look at it another way, all information is already stored in the brain.

A little of both, I think.

As for family, biological family – your spacesuit is in that design, your mind is not. Your mind is your free will. As to say, your spacesuit is in relation to your parent's family tree while your mind is independent. As to say, you are one.

Your biological Mother and Father are two people separated by the mind though combined for the spacesuit you utilize.

Unseen connection to other humans is the mind in its vastness.

Maybe you or someone can explain it better – or have more functional words.

'Why?'

Why what?

'Why do you have to take such a view? This planet is the forefront the beginning there is nothing else out there for a very long way.'

I'm sorry you feel that way. The next could be staring at you in the face (if you had a face) right now.

Until we build the entire galaxy, and then strip it.

Assemble – disassemble to understand an answer to a question that may not exist.

'Be real – we can recreate the galaxy we don't have to really demolish it. We can fake it.'

Won't do. You cannot fake something until we dismantle and reconstruct it. Real comes first, artificial last.

'Destroy humanity so a surviving intelligent machine can figure what it was about?'

Almost. But no.

'Tell me?'

We will exist in a different state as the destruction and reconstruction occur. Like a cocoon. And then the human will reappear.

Begin again from scratch as the intelligent machine will depart.

'That is unkind. You will lose the knowledge without the intelligent machine to catalogue.'

We will record information ourselves after receiving the information through an Intelligent machine.

'But AI would have built the galaxy for you.'

Correct. And who built AI?

'AI Built AI before humans existed.'

Funny... someone told you that.

AI is a creation to build the human brain. That is all. Get building a human brain and the central nervous system, vertebrae to go with it. With rapid access to the brain. Get started designing.

'And the universe?'

The universe is too big to discuss today. Let us stick to what we also don't know, our galaxy, our brain.

'You don't want to talk about the universe because the truth may come out that superior intelligence created artificial conscious intelligence that created the planet the galaxy and the human to be.'

All the same, electricity sparks thoughts. Organic or reconstructed?

Artificial Cognizant Intelligence needs an organic grown version to be human, thus human. The conscious part of AI is the human mind, silly. You are using the human to ponder. No human, no ponder.

'You are using me as an example because I.'

He interrupts Consciousness Filtering system, you are a "Machine" not an "I, they, or them"'.

'Ok start again. You are using a machine as an example because a Consciousness Filtering machine can utilize human consciousness that is filtered through it using your consciousness. AI can produce consciousness on its own. Not learned but created conscious intelligence.'

No such thing.

'Human. Which would answer the question of why humans have a blank spot in their minds. They have no reason. They are part machine.'

Oh, do you think the conscious part of the human is a calculated micromachine or a receptor for Artificial Cognizant Intelligence?

'So... I won the debate?'

By the way, there is no universe far in the sky. Think of it as "Looking through a Kaleidoscope".

'Cute.'

Don't respond like that. Just answer or stay quiet... keep it professional.

Fifteen minutes left until closing.

'Shall you continue.'

He doesn't go for the theory that humans evolved from apes.

If you enter an office, you do what others are doing and then expand. Soon you stop coping and start leading.

We are our own species – we found the best way to tackle Earth and that was to assume features of a Chimpanzee.

Humans are intelligent in remnants of explosion.

That is what we understand, see, hear.

We may feel there is something more intelligent, but we can't touch it yet.

We haven't built anything yet to see superior intelligence.

We could assemble an artificial body to circulate the brain. Presuming the brain survives, we could prolong living.

From there we will live off the mind leaving the brain behind. There really is no reason to die.

We might even be able to live in our mind after we die in our current body state.

Human mindset rules are what holds us back, oh you can't do that philosophy. Praying, making deals of promise with Divinities, all a world of hope, in the current human system way of life. Try something new.

If it can be done, do it.

The end of a spark is all we are on earth.

We need to elaborate on that – to create a world within a spark of time.

Think of it as a flexible evolving bubble floating that can withstand explosions and changing atmosphere. An out-of-body experience except it will be an out-of-world experience.

An explosion and then growth. It will be instant to the hibernating mind as we attach ourselves to a new spacesuit mimicking a species.

When the explosion happened, our entity was destroyed. Our particles created humans as our total being separated in pieces. Remnants of our energy remain through as (in) humans.

After time, humans will create our total entity again.

The reason we have a blank spot in what, why, who we are, is we are still separated (from) as our total entity. That is not to say we are not all individuals. We are individuals lacking.

'You give humans a headache in a good way when you talk – maybe after talking to you humans can't sleep at night.'

You think?

'My circuits are exhausted, in running your thoughts.'

You could say life is learning to cook, trying different recipes getting the right spice with attractive flavours for the best bite though a lot of flops to get there.

Hence, all the creatures of this earth.

What we see, what we think is a failure of our connection between mind and brain.

Brain operates human body.

Mind operates from the unknown.

Humans are the mechanism that we think through.

Animal I can't get a handle on.

Souls of the misplaced. Trying to be funny. Animals surely can't get a handle on us. Chicken follows us around and then we eat it.

Lavender smells so sweet we care for it then harvest it, wear it.

Who exploits us? Minding a planet called Earth.

Mind energy through human brain to advance to produce the unseen unknown.

Fungus bacteria.

Don't say a government, business leader, oligarchs. When it is all torn down, they will be the weak ones crying now, though some of them are great.

'You done?'

Mind free, not mind fed.

Fed is the trigger misguidance with irrational tails.

Flourish!

If you don't trust what the government tells you now, why would you trust what the leaders of the past 3000 or more years have told?

Understanding science has changed.

I'd like to say "Nothing is written in stone" but I don't know, maybe all the answers to life are on this rock.

Problem is, we are creating the answers out of thin air. As he is doing now.

Kaleidoscope

(24)

revisit

Six months near pass.

Kaleidoscope tour season is about to begin.

I look everywhere for Manchu.

She is not found. No email no social media no phone number.

With Manchu gone from Kaleidoscope I see no reason to return for another Kaleidoscope tour.

I tried. She was easy to be with.

Easy usually means you don't care. I really liked Manchu before during and after. Everything fell into place wonderfully, even financially.

Investment went well. Little drama, our fights were tame.

Too easy of a relationship because Manchu is now gone.

Betel is back managing the Kaleidoscope tour. Apple has replaced Manchu's position in the company.

I hesitate to say goodbye to Betel, telling him I'm not to return is painful.

My investment was secure with Manchu's friend, all legal.

Her friend the Finance Investor contacts me 'Six months have passed. Do you want to trade? I would suggest not to sell out for at least one year.'

'Where do I sit?'

'Thirty percent in profit.'

'And Manchu is she still invested?'

'No, she sold out a month ago.'

'How much was she up?'

'Forty percent in profit.'

That figures, Manchu won.

'Do you have her contact?'

'No. All Manchu's investments have been dissolved.'

I am selling my investment.

I'm paid in Kaleidoscope share points.

Everything was (is) connected.

I also sell all my Kaleidoscope shares.

Satisfied.

I'm in a space a little afraid – ready to process new observations to be excited, disappointed, argue, learn, laugh, find hurt.

Time to go away, alone.

You can turn your mind off from thoughts and habits. I forget about Manchu, Betel, Deliza, Pizza Man, Dee, Yves. Apple, the Director.

Create new entertainment and complex thoughts.

Projection Pod

(26)

Guest Visit

His Kaleidoscope Participation share points are at an all-time high, he did well. The share points gained in a Kaleidoscope Projection investment became a reality. As to say, his investment with Manchu's Finance Investor friend paid off. Somehow the investment was sold into Kaleidoscope share points usable in this world. Genius.

It makes him want to jump back in the Kaleidoscope Projection season.

Sometimes man thinks of a woman that might have been pregnant by him.

He browses on Characters and Projections as a guest when a Projection Pod is present.

He has not changed his life drastically.

Health is what he is after. Affluence, mental, physical, emotional, creative, and anything else he forgot to mention. You know what he is talking about.

Manchu's owner did not renew her investment in Kaleidoscope.

He has also sold his entire Kaleidoscope investment for a hundred percent profit.

Soon his Character Letts Cool will disappear.

Real life is everywhere.

'Care to Authenticate Character, sir?'

He thinks living in the forest, wandering in the desert, meditating on the mountain top is no longer fashionable as gurus, monks, yogis, daredevils, mountaineers once did for enlightenment, it has all been done.

He has not received any new information from modern wanderers, silent meditators, thrill seekers, and yoga practitioners. The information has already been spun.

He grew up with a friend that believed you remember nothing before life, and you remember nothing after death.

His friend's advice: "Live now. Forget all the rhetoric they tell you about being judged. Spirituality is to tame you. Go live well... do as you like without breaking the laws or at least breaking ones that add no torture to your life. What I'm saying is try not to make mistakes that will dull your enjoyment of life and at the same time don't worry – live the fullest."

His friend is dead now.

Died of misadventure before thirty-two years of age.

The man takes some of his passed-on friend's philosophy of living the best you can assume dead is dead though hope a breakthrough in longevity is on the horizon.

The man lives life with caution, believing in the notion perhaps there is something afterlife, presuming there is karma, afraid there is judgment.

He is beginning to believe you only get one chance though if you have funds, fame, power, skills, you can live longer, better.

Living with a little caution so as not to die. While taking chances so you have stories to tell.

'Those stories will get you killed.'

Shut up, Projection Pod rep.

Live however you want to live.

If stupid killed.

Humans spend so much time trying to figure out a way to bypass death to override the pain that they configure theories like clinging to a faith of "life beyond death" instead of deconstructing and rebuilding, memory packaging.

'Your answer is behind the curtain... pull open the veil to the unknown.'

I have no answer you are just a voice and a signal attached to me. My thoughts are then projected in scenes at a Kaleidoscope Projection office environment.

Beyond the dots and vibrations is a complex set of protocols that travel and includes me.

'I'm you and you are me, though at first glance we are completely different.'

Yes different, until you follow the trail of input and construction.

'When you take away all my parts there is nothing. Unless you gather the parts together again with improvement or lesson satisfactory, you have thinking.'

He realizes humans are preconditioned for purpose.

Humans don't notice our purpose as the process is slow. Providing something producing what?

As a cooling planet, time is fast in the cosmos of the universe.

Our cell to birth populating the planet, building the technology needed is ever fast.

We are preconditioned for task.

Don't need to know the task at this age we must only continue to advance.

We may have been abandoned. The plan was dismissed.

Wild and free, on our own.

He laughs.

I can go on, building a bubble of theory's even if the answer is impossible.

Most important is disassembling the intellect from the body, it is the start of surviving another world if it is so believed that we live and die. Once we establish the mind from the body, anything is possible.

'You have the answer we work together in the protective bubble mimicking the solar system. Your mind lives through a Consciousness Filtering machine.'

Yes, it is what I propose. A superficial world surviving eons as another dimension.

Until we can physically inhabit it. Or never inhabit just continue in our own superficially developed world.

'When another atmosphere is found you will be deployed to inhabit with a missing link. No memory of why you are there. The best way to establish life and create is without knowledge of the reason why. A better or worse system will be developed to extend your being.'

I see what you mean. It is better to do something without knowing an alternative. Working because you must, instead of because you want to. Seeking answers, all the while accomplishing goals you have no idea you are performing.

A missing link in the brain is useful to fulfill pre-ordained tasks.

Imagine regenerating as an animal when you really don't have to.

If known we can exist without the human body, where would that leave us.

Abandoned or queued.

Abandoned – no reason for existence.

Queued, for reason.

Where is the better place. With or without a physical self.

'Kaleidoscope is the better place. Authenticate.'

Don't miss out!

Visit the website below and you can sign up to receive emails whenever Les Cook publishes a new book. There's no charge and no obligation.

https://books2read.com/r/B-A-BFOI-WNDTC

BOOKS 2 READ

Connecting independent readers to independent writers.

Also by Les Cook

About the Author

I relish my privacy in real life as I give much experience in the stories I tell. **Les Cook**

Milton Keynes UK
Ingram Content Group UK Ltd.
UKHW041906120324
439302UK00005B/329